"My life has been filled with many blessings, and one of them has been my great friendship with Joe Bonsall and the rest of the Oak Ridge Boys. As it turns out, Joe cannot only sing, but he also can write. From My Perspective is filled with wit, charm, and heart, written by one of God's special people."

—George H. W. Bush

"I love this guy! I love his heart! I love his energy! I love the big view of the world that he embraces. But most of all I love him because he has never forgetten his roots, and I admire him so much for that. This will be a great read!"

—Bill Gaither

"Joe Bonsall's From My Perspective is a baby boomer's delight, but hardly limited to us old-timers. There's something for everyone here: nostalgia, patriotism, humor, faith, and a whole lot of music and fun. I've been an Oak Ridge Boys fan for decades, but who knew—until G.I. Joe and Lillie and now From My Perspective— that their award-winning tenor was also a riveting author?"

—**Jerry B. Jenkins,** author and owner of Christian Writers Guild

"Joe has always been a gifted singer and communicator. How great to see him using these gifts on a project with such a positive message."

—Michael W. Smith

"Joe Bonsall is a study in contrasts. I understand contrasts because I received a degree in classical music, Metropolitan Opera style, but most people who know my music think it's more in sync with the Grand Old Opry. So I can understand the contrasts of a young boy who was raised in the concrete jungles of Philly, hearing the sounds of those Philly groups and then migrating to Tennessee. That same man found a new depth within himself, his family, his music and his God on a farm in Tennessee, all the while learning to play a banjo. What a contrast. What a trip! This reflection reveals a man who is not satisfied with staying in one place without making that place more productive. These reflections are a study of more things to come. I can hardly wait!"

—**Duane Allen,** Oak Ridge Boys lead singer

From My Perspective

JOSEPH S. BONSALL

Charlotte, Tennessee 37036

From My Perspective
Copyright © 2010 by Joseph S. Bonsall

Published by Journey Press, a division of Sheaf House Publishers, LLC.
Requests for information should be addressed to:

Editorial Director
Sheaf House Publishers, LLC
3641 Hwy 47 N
Charlotte, TN 37036
jmshoup@sheafhouse.com
www.sheafhouse.com

Library of Congress Control Number: 2010927528

ISBN 978-0-9824832-2-0 (softcover)

Cover Photos by Jarrett Gaza of Jarrett Gaza Photography.
Interior design by John Boegel.

10 11 12 13 14 15 16 17 18 19—10 9 8 7 6 5 4 3 2 1

MANUFACTURED IN THE UNITED STATES OF AMERICA

CONTENTS

AMERICA

FAITH

BONUS SHORT STORY

DEDICATION

This book is dedicated
to **Miss Lo-Dee Hammock,**
a dear friend
who is always there for me.
She is my second mother!

From the fullness of His grace we have all received one
blessing after another. John 1:16, NIV

Sing unto him a new song; play skillfully with a loud noise.
Psalm 33:3, KJV

FOREWORD

I first met Joe and the rest of the Boys at a show many years ago in Myrtle Beach, South Carolina. We were having a reunion of World War II pilots, most of whom were from my squadron, and we all decided to go see the Oak Ridge Boys sing on a Saturday night at the Alabama Theater. And the Oak Ridge Boys let us in free as a thank you for our service! At that time I had no idea how much respect the group had for guys like me. Then I met them face-to-face. I can tell you . . . they are the real deal.

We became friends from that night on, and my love and respect for them has only grown over the years. My wife, Victoria, and I try not to miss them when they are performing nearby, and I have introduced them from the stage many times. I will never forget them singing at my eightieth birthday party. Now that was a party!

I first realized that Joe could write when he sent me a manuscript of his book G.I. Joe and Lillie several years back. Again, his love and respect for veterans shined brightly in that book, as it does in From My Perspective. But this book is much more. In it Joe covers a lot of ground, and every chapter takes you on a ride of its own. Of course, he writes about his love for America and its vets, but he also takes the reader on quite a few other trips—all from Joe's perspective. Inspiring and funny at times—it is often thought provoking and emotional. Heck, he even writes about cats and barn swallows.

I think at the heart and soul of this book, though, is Joe Bonsall himself, a young man who grew up in Philadelphia with a set of World War II veteran parents who taught him to love this country and those who have sacrificed much for the freedom we all enjoy. He was taught that if he worked hard and stayed honest with everyone, he could succeed. And he has, as an author and singer, a husband, dad, and granddad. Writing a book is not easy. I know. I have written a few. I am proud of Joe for this unique piece of work. I am proud to call him a friend.

~ **General Chuck Yeager**
www.chuckyeager.com

FROM MY PERSPECTIVE
An Introduction

Hello, readers, both constant and new, and welcome to this book of commentaries and short stories you now hold in your hand. I am thankful to Sheaf House Publishers, Joan Shoup and Joy DeKok, for putting this project on track. I am also very thankful for my long-time friend, associate, and book agent, Kathy Harris, for coming up with the concept for this book. Thanks, as always, to my long-time friend and counsel S. Gary Spicer for caring that Joseph is doing the right things right! Thanks to my friends Lo-Dee Hammock and Darrick Kinslow for constant encouragement. I would be remiss not to say thank you to my wonderful wife, Mary Ann Bonsall, for without her . . . I am nothing.

I pray these writings will be entertaining as well as thought provoking and, on many levels, a blessing to your life for having shared the moment.

For the last thirty-seven years my middle name has been "of the," meaning "of the Oak Ridge Boys." The accomplishments as well as the sheer staying power of this quintessential American music group have been a mind-boggling experience as I have watched every dream I have ever dreamed come true. Along with my singing partners, Duane Allen, William Lee Golden, and Richard Sterban, I have seen the world and conquered every aspect of the music business. Bottom line: We sing songs for a living, and God has blessed our creative efforts over and over again in every way possible. Our group is feeling good, singing good, and still playing over 150 shows a year. We are making new and challenging music, even though we are no longer the young kids on the block.

We have raised families, put kids through college, and have made it possible for those around us to do the same. I have been blesssed with a wonderful and beautiful wife, Mary, two grown daughters,

9

Jennifer and Sabrina, two hard-working sons-in-law, Dan and Mark, and two precious grandchildren, Breanne and Luke.

I am very thankful for my sixty plus years on this planet. I would say blessed beyond deserving, but aren't we all?

I am writing this little introduction from Kennebunkport, Maine, where the Oak Ridge Boys and Girls are the guests of former President George Herbert Walker Bush and his incredible wife, former First Lady Barbara Bush.

If you have read the book I wrote on the Oaks, titled An American Journey and published by New Leaf Press, then you are well aware of our long-time friendship with these great Americans. I wrote an entire chapter about this precious friendship called "Kennebunkport Memoir." Most of the high points of my life have happened as a direct result of knowing President Bush #41.

I find myself writing and at the same time staring at the beautiful northern Atlantic Ocean as the tide slowly rolls in. The sun sparkles, shines, reflects, and dances upon the relatively still sea. The rugged shoreline stretches out as far as one can see in both directions. Lobster boats are visible in the distance in silhouette against the sun's stunning glare.

Behind me stands an historic home that has seen decades of world leaders and dignitaries dine and sleep and meet within its walls. I feel so blessed to be here. So honored. Walkers Point, Maine, is a long way from 3517 Jasper Street in the Kensington neighborhood of Philadelphia, where a young Joey walked the streets at night and dreamed about days just like this one.

It would seem that most of my life has taken place a long way from the Philly streets, where I lived for nineteen years. And yet those streets and those childhood memories are perhaps the biggest part of what I have come to be. I learned to win and I learned to lose. I learned to fight and I learned how to run away from a fight. I learned how to get along with people of every race and creed. People talk about America being a melting pot. I assure you each neighborhood in Philly was a big pot for certain. I will not say that it all melted just right, but who can say that today? We all keep trying!

I had a job from the time I was nine years old. I stocked shelves, carried groceries home for people, ran errands, carried cases of soda and beer into basements, worked as a short order cook, an office mailroom boy, and a veterinarian's assistant. I eventually worked my way up to being a sales-order representative for a major sugar company. That last job was fast-paced and fun, and the office was filled with pretty girls . . . but it wasn't singing. Jack Frost Sugar Corporation was even willing to put me through college and move me on up in the company, but I turned them down and joined the Keystones at age nineteen. I have never been sorry. Now there is no Jack Frost Sugar, but Joey is still singing!

I put on shows in my back bedroom like you would not believe, using a dust mop and a small lampshade for a microphone and stand, while Elvis or the Statesmen Quartet rang out from my little stereo set. I had the moves, baby. I was rocking!

I was a street hoodlum for several years, and later on I was the president of my high school Bible club. I have hung out on street corners with the worst kinds of characters. I have been active in Christian Endeavor and Youth for Christ.

I have ignored the Lord and thankfully embraced the Lord.

I have starved and I have prospered. I have cried and I have laughed myself into comas. I have loved and have been loved. I have been blessed and have strived to be a blessing.

I spent my younger days in a perpetual dream state, hoping and praying that one day I would leave the streets and sing. I hoped that perhaps I might eventually find the right people to occupy the same circumference of being as little Joey. Now that all these things have come to pass and the years have turned into decades, I find myself reflective and creative concerning my life, and more then ever I tend to write things down.

So I give you a variety of little stories and musings in this book. I am not sure why some might want to read about just one man's perspective, but if you have gotten this far, then you are still with me. I pray that you will enjoy what you read and that, as much as possible, you will be blessed and entertained by the words.

Unlike performing onstage with the Oak Ridge Boys, I find writing to be a very personal and individual experience. One writes alone, just as one reads alone, and what a joy it is when the written words find a connection to those who take the time to read it. I have experienced this feeling and personal connection over and over again with the amazing success of my book *G.I. Joe and Lillie.*

From My Perspective

Your author is a man who loves music, loves to write, loves his family, loves his friends, loves being an Oak Ridge Boy, loves nature, loves America, loves veterans and those who sacrifice for our freedom, loves his banjo, loves the Phillies, loves birds, loves cats, loves to laugh, and most of all loves Jesus Christ.

You will find a bit of all of these things in the pages ahead. So pull up a chair and spend a little time with Joseph S. Bonsall. I am really just a simple man who has been down a lot of different roads and is willing to share a small portion of his life with you. You might call it . . . one man's perspective!

God bless each one of you, and thanks for being here!

Photo courtesy of Jarrett Gaza

Photo courtesy of Kathy Gangwisch

MUSIC

WHEN I WAS ELVIS

For several years little Joey was actually Elvis Presley. At least I thought I was. I had all his singles and most of his record albums, including movie soundtracks like *Girls, Girls, Girls, Blue Hawaii, It Happened at the Worlds Fair*, and *G.I. Blues*. I knew every word to every song too.

When I went to the movies to see *Love Me Tender* or *Loving You* or *King Creole*, I could picture myself in the part just as easily as the King. I was even sneering in my high school graduation photo. Man, he looked good, sang good, and got all the girls. That would be me one day. Of this I was certain!

I once made up a story of Elvis' obscure twin named Eesley, who filled in whenever the King took a rest. Eesley Presley was little Joey, of course. Always ready to go. Weird when I found out one day that he actually had a twin brother who died at childbirth. Hmm . . .

Actually, from a musical standpoint, growing up in Philly in the mid fifties and early sixties was very cool as well as inspiring. A lot of entertainers came out of Philly, such as Chubby Checker, Frankie Avalon, Fabian, Paul Anka, Freddy "Boom Boom" Cannon, and scores of others. *American Bandstand* and Dick Clark also came out of Philadelphia.

A neighbor girl named Cathy Stathius and I used to go down to *American Bandstand* often and stand in line around 68th and Market. We would get in there a lot of times too. It was a blast to jitterbug in front of the three cameras with Dick Clark standing in the corner of the studio. I was always amazed at how small the room was. It looked huge on television.

A side story: When the Oak Ridge Boys started to come on strong in the late seventies, word got out that I used to be on *Bandstand*.

Then it got out that I was a regular on *Bandstand*. That wasn't true, of course, as I was only on there a few times. As years went by, Dick Clark and I became friends, and he asked me to write a piece for the *Twenty Fifth Anniversary of American Bandstand* book. I wrote about three pages on what it was like to go down there and not get in. He then made me an "honorary regular." But to all those folks who used to watch *American Bandstand*, I seriously doubt you ever saw little Joey doing the Peppermint Twist or Bristol Stomping all over poor little Cathy Stathius.

How cool it is now to have been voted into the Philadelphia Alliance Music Hall of Fame, along with Oaks' bass singer Richard Sterban, who is from Camden, New Jersey, right across the river. My name is now in stone, right there with all of my Philly music heroes. Hall and Oates, the Stylistics . . . Joe Bonsall. Huh?

Back to my story. At the tender age of eighteen years, my feeble attempt to be just like the King came to a screeching halt in a Philly suburb. I will explain.

By then, I was singing with the Faith Four Quartet, and we were doing pretty well for a little part-time gospel band. We traveled on weekends and made it back to work by Monday.

Well, one Saturday night we found ourselves booked at the big gospel concert that was held twice a year in the Souderton Pennsylvania High School auditorium. I had been to many quartet shows in Souderton, and for my little group to be playing on that stage with two major acts was really exciting and a very big deal. The Faith Four consisted of me singing tenor, Ron Graeff on lead, Bernie "The Head" Clampfer on baritone, Bradley Walker singing bass, and a part-time piano player named Wayne Mullen from Maple Shade, New Jersey.

We weren't all that great, but we tried hard and we loved to sing. Up to this point we had only played in churches and a few youth camp meetings, so we were all stoked about the big-time show in Souderton. We even bought ourselves some new suits for the event. All five us went down to South Philadelphia to this cheapo suit place and bought mint green sharkskin numbers complete with matching ties.

On that Saturday morning before driving up to Souderton, I felt I needed to do more. After all, this was the big time. So I bought some black hair dye and proceeded to make a mess of the bathroom, coloring my hair jet black so I could look a bit more like Elvis Presley. My hair ended up so darn black it appeared to be blue. I combed it up into the highest pompadour one could possibly imagine and locked it in tight with a whole can of mom's Aqua-Net hairspray. I then proceeded to mold a nice, attractive little ducktail thing in the back. Now . . . I was, oh, so ready to go! I was even sneering a bit. The big lip was working for me. I was looking good.

That night when the master of ceremonies called our name, five nervous young boys in mint green suits from Krass Brothers on South Street hit the stage. It was incredibly hot up there, and we were giving it our best when sometime during the third song, which was ironically called "That's Enough," I looked to my left and Ronnie Graeff had stopped singing. He was pointing and trying not to laugh at the fact that my hair had actually melted and long streams of sweaty black dye were streaming down my whole face. Dye was dripping onto the shoulders of my mint green suit and had ruined my fancy tie. It was just horrible. It would not stop! I ran offstage and wiped most of it off, made a joke about it, and kept on singing. But I was almost in tears. Our whole stand was only twenty minutes, but that last song or two felt like a day and a half.

Well, that ended my Elvis fixation for good. I figured that, for better or worse, from here on out I had better stick to being just Joe Bonsall!

Addendum

In the year of 1977, people were starting to see the Oak Ridge Boys as more than just a controversial and cutting edge gospel group. We were becoming bona-fide country music stars. Our little song "Y'all Come Back Saloon" was screaming up the charts and real success for the Oaks was beginning to take shape.

On August 16 of that magical year, we were heading north on Interstate 65 through Kentucky, and our tour bus was just rocking. Everyone was laughing and cutting up, because lots of good stuff was going on for us. I was sitting in the jump seat beside our long-time driver Harley Pinkerman. Harley's CB radio was crackling away with "10-4's" and "hey, good buddies." In the background, Jackson Brown music was blaring on the front lounge speakers.

I remember hearing some trucker say something about Elvis, and seeing old Harley's face change. He steered the bus to the shoulder of the interstate and shut it all down. He got out of his seat and stared blankly at all of us, who were by now sensing that something was awry. We turned off Jackson Brown and gave Harley the floor.

"Boys, I hate to tell you all this, but Elvis Presley has died."

The years have revealed that Elvis had a rough time at the end. His personal life was a mess. He was overweight and taking drugs to go up, drugs to come down, and drugs to go sidewise. Handfuls of that stuff took him all the way down, as it so often does.

I loved the man and I loved his music. I even loved a few of his movies. I saw him in person six times, and the show was always just incredible. I actually met him for one quick moment in Memphis in 1969. I was singing with the Keystones, and William Lee Golden and Duane Allen of the Oak Ridge Boys had invited us to sing at the National Quartet Convention. Elvis and his wife Priscilla were at the side of the stage, watching the gospel groups sing. He did love gospel music.

I was in awe of him. Even today when my iPod Shuffle lands on an old Elvis song, I have to smile as I picture little Joey in his bedroom wanting to be just like him. I still know every word to every song. But the big E only made it to age forty-two, while little Joey is now in his sixties and still singing and breathing oxygen . . . so happy now that I did not end up being just like Elvis!

Photo by Eddie Beesley

TAYLOR

As of this writing, the hottest property in the music world is our Hendersonville, Tennessee, neighbor Taylor Swift. Miss Swift is a nineteen-year-old beauty, who has stunned the universe with her songwriting and incredible stage performance. With a presence and a charisma that seems way beyond her years, she has won every award there is to win, and her music sales are stratospheric. She has put a charge into Nashville much the way Garth Brooks did in the nineties. I am very proud of her. Her songs are geared to a much younger audience then me, although I listen to it more than you might think. Turning fifteen and being told I love you by a guy who lied is more my granddaughter Breanne's cup of tea. But I still say, "Go, Taylor!" I love it when good people win!

I am never one to jump right onboard a bandwagon, so I will admit to being a little slow appreciating our hometown superstar, Taylor Swift. Yes, she lives right here in good old Hendersonville, Tennessee, which is very cool.

When she first came on the scene, I thought her music to be a bit teenybopper, bubble gum, and I did not pay as much attention. But I am paying attention now, and here is why.

I recently attended several big music events in Las Vegas with the Oak Ridge Boys, and Taylor played a major role in each show, the Academy of Country Music Awards, and the taping of a George Strait tribute. I talked with her briefly backstage and sat just a few seats from her at both events. It is hard not to pay attention to Taylor Swift.

The girl is, indeed, young and beautiful and seems full of music. There is also a unique energy that fills the air around her. Some of this energy is typical teenager for certain, but it goes much deeper than that. She seems to be on constant high idle, ready to go, willing to do whatever it takes to succeed. There exists a magic and a drive that goes way beyond her years.

After meeting her I took the time to give a hard listen to her newest award-winning album, *Fearless,* and a light came on. This girl is indeed a prodigy. A genius, perhaps. Much like a young Bruce Springsteen, who came out of high school writing songs about growing up in the city, Taylor captures the life of a young girl growing up in an American small town. Her songs are well crafted, and her performance of these songs flies right out of her soul.

When you take in the fact that she was somewhat of a loner in high school, her success is even more mind boggling. The young Taylor was paying attention and, like a great poet, she went home every night and wrote it all down. Now the world is listening.

I am proud of Taylor Swift, and I think the coming years will bring forth more and more excellence in her singing and in her writing. I believe she will be around for a long time, and it will be fun to witness her continual rise within stardom as everyone takes notice of the deeply rooted talent she possesses. Music. Books. Movies. The sky is the limit for Miss Swift.

I recently read where she asked the Hendersonville High School dance squad to take part in her new video. I would not be surprised to see a Taylor Swift High School here someday. God bless her and keep her focused and safe. She is our neighbor, and we wish her well.

I am now onboard the bandwagon!

THE THURSDAY NIGHT PICKIN' CIRCLE

The farm and acreage Mary and I own sit right on the Kentucky-Tennessee border. In fact, the state line runs right in front of the house. The house sits back a bit from the foot of the driveway that leads down into the holler. The holler is the centerpiece of the property. I like to tell people that they can eat dinner in Tennessee and go to bed in Kentucky; however, that is somewhat of a stretch because our humble home actually sits entirely in the Commonwealth of Kain-tuck-ee!

Geographically speaking, we actually live in the small town of Bugtussle, Kentucky.

Lafayette, Tennessee, is fourteen miles to the southwest of us, and the Monroe County seat of Tomkinsville, Kentucky, is approximately fourteen miles northeast of us. However, in between my farm and T'Ville as the locals call it, sits the little town of Gamaliel, Kentucky. That is where this little story takes place.

Now Gamaliel is about seven miles from our farm in the Bugtussle holler and is pronounced Ga-mail-ya (although someone just passing through could never guess that). It looks like Ga-ma-leel . . . or ga-mell . . . or Ga-meal. anything but Ga-mail-ya.

My neighbor Harold runs a convenience store and gas station in Gamaliel, right next to the Dollar General. There are also a small IGA store, a Farmers Supply Depot, and several restaurants, which feature either barbecue or good, down-home country cooking—meat and three's, as they are known in the South.

Mary and I and the grandkids just love to drive up to the Gamaliel Diner for a big, country breakfast, featuring the finest pancakes in Kentucky! Then we will usually fill up my diesel containers at Harold's store, top off the truck, and pick up some sweet feed for my donkeys and corn for my deer at the farm supply.

Right next to the aforementioned Gamaliel Diner, there is a furniture store. Across the street are a bank and the brand new elementary school. This school, like the relatively new Monroe County Junior and Senior High Schools in T'Ville, were built by our tax dollars and grants from the Kentucky State Lottery. Nice to see that all those losing Powerball tickets account for something, and anyone will tell you these schools are beautiful.

To the left of the bank, sitting back a few yards from the road, is the city hall/senior center, and that is where I spent almost four hours of my life this past Thursday evening. I had always heard that a bunch of old pickers gathered there on Thursdays, and I had always meant to stop by. But two things have prevented me from doing so. The Oaks schedule and—I will admit it—I was chicken. Well, actually, just not confident enough in my banjo playing to enter a room full of pickers and sit in on the jam. However, this past week I was in town on Thursday, I was at the farm, and I was actually feeling pretty good about my playing!

I had run out to the farm the night before because I had some equipment coming in from John Deere that had been serviced for me. Tractors and cutters and weed eaters and Gators all prepared and ready for the rest of 2006. I spent the rest of that afternoon cleaning up flood debris from three pastures. It is important to at least get the big wood off the fields so when grass starts growing they are not concealed. That can be a disaster for a rotary cutter blade later in the year.

Now, good old Salt Lick Creek will flood again several times this spring, I am certain, and that is why I don't try to get every little thing cleaned up. These are huge pastures so just the big stuff is handled—like a tree trunk or huge branches or a family of four sitting at a breakfast table.

I dragged myself into the house around 4 p.m., took a shower, and called Mary who was in Hendersonville nursing a bad cold. I told her I was considering running up to Gamaliel and pickin' at the city hall, and she encouraged me to do so.

"You have always wanted to do it, so go on," she said. "I will see you in the morning."

The approval of the wife is always important!

So I threw the old banjer in the truck and drove on up to Gam-ale-ya—yet a different phonetic spelling!

I could hear the pickin' as I was walking up the steps, and the volume sort of grew to a crescendo when I opened the door. What a sound it was! Sitting there in a big circle were senior citizens, men and woman, all pickin' and singin'. I would guess there were about ten guitar players, three mandolins, four fiddles, and one wonderful old banjo player.

It was just beautiful.

Sitting all around behind the circle were groups of people who were eating snacks and listening. After the song they all looked at me. Many recognized me as one "of the," however, most did not.

Someone said, "Well, son, just put some money in the cup, sign in, and pull up a chair."

There was a long table filled with all kinds of food and drinks. Kind of like a potluck church social.

I put some money in the Styrofoam cup, signed my name on the sheet, grabbed a folding chair, and placed it strategically across from Mr. Ray, who had been pickin' banjer for over fifty years. He immediately became my hero.

I am just a student and a work in progress who has been playing banjo for only three years, four months, twelve days, and about six hours. I thanked everyone for the sincere welcome and promised not to get in the way.

My fifty-eight years made me, by far, the youngest one in the room except for a young boy of about nine years old. He didn't sing or pick but would break out into a dancing jig every once in a while, much to the delight of all.

Everyone took turns singing. Most of the singing and playing was really quite good (and some of it was really not). However, the feeling that was put into every note of every song should be witnessed by every jaded professional musician on the planet.

Everything was so informal. Someone would say, "How about 'Bile Them Cabbage Down,' " and a fiddle player would yell, "Key of A," proceed to kick it off, and away we would all go. I was able to hold my own pretty good on "Foggy Mountain Breakdown," "Cripple Creek," "Cumberland Gap," and most all of the gospel songs. I even took a little solo ride on "Poor Reuben" in D tuning, which I have been practicing for months. But other than that, I would just find a little texture roll or stroke a lick or two or just chunk and watch Mr. Ray, whose old fingers danced up and down the neck like Earl himself. Sometimes one would sing alone and other times everyone sang—in full voice, too! It was something to behold.

It went on and on.

"Sing one, Doris!"

"Okay . . . 'Looking for a City' in G." Then Doris would hammer on her guitar and take off singing.

"How 'bout you, Jim?"

"All right, then . . . how 'bout a little 'Rollin' in My Sweet Baby's Arms,' key of E."

Boom—away everyone went, following Jim's lead vocal and mandolin in E!

Conversation:

"What kind of banjo is that, son?"

"It's a Deering, sir."

"Well, Stelling does make a fine banjer."

"Well, this one is a Deering. It's their top-of-the-line Tenbrooks model, sir."

"Yessiree bob, my own daddy played a Stelling. Sounds good!"

What fun!

The highlight of the night, though, was when a very elderly fiddle player who must have been close to ninety started to play "Blue Moon of Kentucky." He slowly stood up and began to fiddle. For a while everyone just listened to him play, but eventually everyone joined in pickin'. The tempo was slow and reverent.

Then someone started to sing and soon everyone in the room was singing, including the folks who were gathered in chairs in the corner or standing along the wall, and even those who were making sandwiches at the food table. The emotion was overwhelming. There was not a dry eye in the room. In fact, tears were actually flowing down people's cheeks. The song lasted for a good ten minutes, and when it ended you could have heard a pin drop.

An old fellow cradling a mandolin turned to me and asked, "Did you ever get to meet Bill Monroe?"

I said, "Yes, sir, on quite a few occasions. In fact, the Oak Ridge Boys once recorded a version of 'Blue Moon of Kentucky' with him and his Bluegrass Boys."

It was if I told him that I had just bought him a condo in Fort Myers or that, perhaps, I had in my possession a secret potion that might heal that arthritis in his picking hand. He got up, grabbed me by the shoulders, and hugged me.

"I just loved that man," he whispered. "Must have been a real honor for you!"

I assured him through my own tears that it was indeed.

I stayed there in the pickin' circle for four hours. Once in a while a few would leave and a few different ones would come in and take their place, but around ten o'clock or so, more and more folks were putting their instruments in their cases, grabbing a snack, and heading for home.

I gave Mr. Ray a set of John Pearse strings for his banjo. Most of our bunch uses these strings, and I thought he might enjoy them. He shook my hand and said, "Come on back and pick with us again sometime!"

I assured him that I would.

Those gathered in the pickin' circle played music as it is supposed to be played. From the heart and from the soul and for the sheer enjoyment of playing, no matter how technically correct it may or may not have been. I believe that is why God gave us music to begin with. I am certain that even ol' David must have hit a clam or two on his little harp. Well . . . maybe not!

Fact is, I will never forget these fine people for letting me be a part of their world for a night. I fear that many of these old folks may not have many Thursday nights left, but who can make that call. I may not have many left either.

Over the rest of this year, I am quite certain that, God willing, I will spend a lot of my Thursday evenings singing my heart out with the Oak Ridge Boys. Perhaps in your own town. But rest assured, a piece of my heart will be in Gamaliel, Kentucky, at the city hall, sitting in a big pickin' circle with some of the finest people I have ever met.

May God bless every one of them.

Kick one off on the banjer, Mr. Ray!

AN UPDATE AND A LOOK BACK

It began with a call from William Lee Golden late in the summer of 2000. In this day and age of e-mail, we don't use the phone much anymore, so I was a bit surprised to hear it ring. And I was even more surprised at what he told me.

"Joey, I just found out that we are going to be inducted into the Gospel Music Hall of Fame! They said it was for our contributions over all these years."

What an incredible blessing! What a surprise! What an honor!

Interesting timing too. We were in the process of planning and working on *From the Heart*, our first gospel album in over twenty-five years. What a coincidence, if one believes in that sort of thing. I, however, believe it was truly a part of God's plan and His hand of direction upon our lives.

I hung up the phone and immediately thanked my Lord. Then for a long while I just sat on my front porch and gazed out over the green pastures and tree lines of my little piece of Tennessee. I felt very emotional about it all. More so than I could have ever imagined. Later on I found out that each of my singing partners had experienced the same exact feelings.

I shut my eyes and let my mind's eye take a good, hard look back over many years. I saw a young Philly boy at his first gospel singing. A fifteen-year-old future thug who really needed a life change. I could see the Couriers, Cathedrals, Blackwoods, Statesmen, and Speers. I could hear the power harmony and the message that eventually changed my life and led me to Christ. I saw the early days of singing: vans, cars pulling U-Hauls, camp meeting grounds, record racks, and sound sets. I could see church services, high school auditoriums, old buses, quartet suits, no money at all and yet always enjoying every minute of *singing*.

I could see the Oaks in all stages of our career: singing, starving, singing, laughing, singing, crying, singing, riding, singing, flying, singing on and on and on. Yes, always singing, no matter what. Hanging tough, persevering, giving all of ourselves in every performance every night, whether singing for two hundred folks or twenty thousand. That was the Oak Ridge Boys' way.

Even after all these years, I still feel the same about hitting the stage every night in whatever town and city we are playing. I believe that is one of the reasons we are still around today, traveling and singing and *being* the Oaks! However, it didn't start with us. To really understand the Oak Ridge Boys and what we are all about, you must look back a bit into the past. The Oak Ridge Boys have a very interesting history that dates back to the early 1940s. It is a history steeped in the tradition of Southern-style gospel music.

William Lee Golden first joined the Oaks in 1965, replacing Jim Hamill, who had replaced Gary McSpadden in 1964, who had replaced Ron Page in 1962. Duane Allen joined the group in 1966, after singing for a year with the Prophets Quartet. He replaced Smitty Gatlin. Richard Sterban started singing bass for us in 1972, replacing Noel Fox who had replaced Herman Harper. Richard had been with the Stamps Quartet and the Keystones before that. I joined in 1973, replacing one of the most popular tenors ever, Willie Wynn. Richard and I had previously sung together for years up North in the Keystones.

Although the four of us are the ones America identifies as the Oak Ridge Boys, we owe much to those who held the banner high long before any of us became members. Each of us has the unique experience of being huge fans of the Oaks long before we ever joined.

As a gospel disc jockey in 1964, Duane Allen chartered a bus full of listeners from his hometown in Taylortown, Texas, and took them to a performance of the Oaks in Fort Worth. From the time a young Bill Golden from Brewton, Alabama, first heard the Oak Ridge Boys' old Warner Brothers album *Folk-Minded Spirituals for Spiritual-Minded Folk*, he saw himself as a member of the group. As young singers from the Philadelphia area, Richard and I pretty much believed the Oaks were the most innovative and energetic group we had ever seen, and we still cannot believe we eventually became a vital part of the group's history.

At a show in Missouri a few years ago, eighty-two-year-old Lon Deacon Freeman joined us on stage to sing a few gospel songs. "The Deacon" was a member of the original Oak Ridge Quartet out of Knoxville, Tennessee, in the 1940s and into the 1950s. Back then the group played the Grand Ole Opry and started the original All Night Singings at the Ryman. Their bluegrass-styled, four-part harmonies were loved throughout the South.

So there I was, a twenty-five-year member of a group, singing onstage with an eighty-two-year-old man who had sung in the same group years ago. Wow! After the show "the Deacon" said, "Well, one thing hasn't changed. The Oak Ridge Boys always did rock the house!"

Somewhat mind-boggling, it was one of the greatest nights I can remember as an Oak. Perhaps someday some younger guys will keep this tradition going and maybe an eighty-two-year-old Joe Bonsall will join them on stage and rock the house! Hey, it could happen!

We take this history to the stage each night, and although our music has expanded quite a bit over the years and we do not make our living on the gospel music circuit anymore, one cannot deny the influence of that Southern gospel, four-part harmony in each song we sing—no matter what the genre may be. Just listen to a few Oaks' standards like "Dig a Little Deeper in the Well," "Everyday, You're the One," "Touch a Hand," "It Takes a Little Rain" and "Thank God for Kids," to name a few.

It is always gospel music that reflects our roots and our beginnings. And gospel music is the address where our heritage resides. To a man, we can honestly say it is still and will always be our first love.

I Miss My Banjo
(A silly poem!)

I sit here alone in the Laughlin night
The mighty Colorado rushes by
I miss my banjo

We sing our songs by the riverside
All the while I cry inside
I miss my banjo

Oh, I miss my wife. I miss my cats
Never a doubt about any of that
I miss my banjo

It's not that I know how to play
It sounds like ka ka some might say
I miss my banjo

My cats are happy and so is Timmer
But soon my finger picks will simmer
I miss my banjo

I dream of opening up the case
And driving all my friends away
I miss my banjo

Plenty of time to pick for me
When I get back home to Tennessee
But for now
I miss my banjo

THE JOURNEY

"The Journey" is the title of a song written by your author and recorded by the Oak Ridge Boys for a bluegrass, acoustic-driven collection of songs. The album released in the late summer of 2004 on the Spring Hill label. The story behind how this song came to be seems worthy of a few paragraphs because it is more than just a song. It is a journey in and of itself.

My interest in bluegrass music and banjo playing has been an ongoing experience for the last few years. I decided that I wanted to write a bluegrass gospel song and struggled with idea after idea. Each set of lyrics and melody would lead me to another. Oft times I would just hit a brick wall and give up.

I don't really do a lot of songwriting, but I do have a way with words to a point. And when an idea manifests itself in my head I can usually follow it through in due time to a finished project of some sort. That was the problem with this song idea. It wasn't a complete idea. I constantly found my thoughts scattered all over the place in trying to write a simple little bluegrass tune. So I gave up on it.

Fast forward to Thursday, February 12. I woke up at my farm and found myself a bit reflective about so many friends and loved ones who have passed on in the last few years. I stared at a picture of my mom and dad for a long while and wondered how they were doing.

I thought of John and June, Jake and Vestal, Noel and Lana, Randy and Irene. Good people. Good friends. Now gone on to be with Jesus. In the quietness and solitude of the moment, I knelt down and said a simple prayer. I asked God to look over these dear ones and somehow let them know that they were loved and missed.

I have a small three-stringed mountain instrument called a McNally Strumstick, an amazing little piece of work that sounds much like a dulcimer and is very easy to play. The promotional material at www.strumstick.com will tell you that there are no wrong notes on this instrument, but I assure you I have found a few. However, not on this crisp February morning.

I picked up the Strumstick and picked out a melody that began to haunt me as I played it. I walked all around the house for several hours, playing this melody over and over. In my mind I could hear other instruments, such as fiddle and mandolin, playing with me. It was somewhat mystical in its repetition.

Then words began to come, and I started writing them down. It was as if God were saying to me, "Go on, write about death, but write about the glory and promise of life beyond the grave."

Some of the words I had written over the months seemed to make sense to me now, but there was more to say, and within an hour I wrote five verses. I was pretty happy with them.

I called Jeff Douglas, who has a great little studio at his house, and implored him to call the band and set up a demo session for Friday afternoon. Then I drove to our home in Hendersonville with lyrics in hand and a new appreciation for my little Strumstick.

When I sang my new song for my wife, Mary, she suggested that the first verse could be improved. A few lines that contained *sheep*, *shepherds,* and such seemed a bit overused. Immediately I knew she was right. (This is why I pay her the big bucks!)

I went downstairs and rewrote the first verse. A light came on, and I made it right.

I am in darkness . . . demons are beckoning . . . I am falling . . . am I dreaming?? I am dying . . . Oh, Father, please help me.

"The Journey" moves forward in the second verse when a door just seems to open and the darkness turns to light, and I find myself in the presence of the Savior, who takes me on to heaven.

I was finally very happy with the beginning and middle, but I wanted the last verse to represent more of a challenge. When I awoke Friday morning, February 13, I rewrote it from scratch.

My brother . . . you could die today . . . Are you ready? Are you born again? Only Jesus can lead us past the grave when the final journey's done!

Now I had a song, but the magic was just beginning.

At Jeff's studio my road warrior buddies and I gathered in a circle and played the song over and over again. There was Ryan on fiddle, Donnie on guitar, Jimmy on acoustic bass, Chris on mandolin, and a twelve-year-old dulcimer champion named Sarah Musgrave, who helped us maintain the mountain feel needed for "The Journey."

I played my Strumstick and a little banjo. With the engineering help of Ronnie Fairchild, I now had a CD in my hand that contained the words and melody I had just finished hours ago.

The Oaks left town on February 14 to perform two shows in Clinton, North Carolina. I told them about the song, but I didn't want them to hear the mix until I added some vocals.

In fact, I wrote this in a general e-mail to everybody about the upcoming song selections: "I have a gospel mountain bluegrass song that I have demoed called 'The Journey.' Personally, I am very excited about this song and I look forward to everyone's input."

The next day, February 15, I went back to Jeff's, while Chris Golden and Jimmy Fulbright added harmony to each voice. Ronnie did a final mix and "The Journey" was a reality.

Would the rest of the Oaks share this vision?

For the Oak Ridge Boys to record a song, all four guys must love it and have their total heart and soul into the process of making it a part of our lives. Because a song that is recorded and performed by this group is very meaningful and never taken for granted, the bar is always set very high and the criteria is without measure. It must move us. We all must *love* it!

February 16. I only had a few copies of the demo. Chris Golden asked me to drop one off at his house. Chris loved the song and was so excited. His enthusiasm for the work meant the world to me. Duane Allen asked me to drop a copy by his house. Because we had a lot of great songs, if mine was to be considered at all, I needed to get it into the process. We started recording that week!

Mary and I decided to go out to the farm for a few days, so I dropped a copy in Chris's mailbox. Then I drove by Duane's home and left a copy in his mailbox. We proceeded to the farm, where I would spend a few days working on a fallen tulip poplar tree and grading my driveway.

That evening I received a call from co-producer Michael Sykes. "Hey man, Duane just played me your song over the phone. Congratulations, Joe. I had goose bumps all over the place. It sets the peg for this project, my friend. I think the song is anointed, my brother."

He went on and on and I almost fainted.

Then a call from the ace, Duane Allen.

"Joseph . . . the song is wonderful. It really works. It will make a great cut on the album. I am proud of you."

I cried my eyes out. In fact I was up all night. I was howling louder than the coyotes!

In the meantime, Chris took the song to William Lee, and he also loved it. In fact, his support was overwhelming! He became an ambassador for "The Journey." I found it all a bit overwhelming.

February 18. At a song meeting with Michael and all of the Boys in our office, Richard heard the song for the first time and smiled.

"Wow, that is really good. Way to go, man!"

That made it unanimous. "The Journey" would be a part of the new album! William Lee then took it upon himself to take it downtown and play it for the label.

Phil Johnson, head of A&R at Spring Hill, told me he thought it was a great song and the message would move a lot of hearts. He was glad we were recording it.

Thursday, February 19. Emerald Tracking Room. Michael Sykes and Duane Allen assembled some of the finest pickers in Nashville to lay tracks on the first six songs of the new project. At approximately 7 p.m., after eating just about all the sushi at Koto's restaurant, we gathered as one and recorded "The Journey."

In listening to this song, when the fiddle begins to drone the mountain bluegrass Celtic introduction and you start to hear and feel the lyrics, perhaps you can look back upon this journey. The journey of a simple little song that I believe was given to me by the Lord.

I give Him the praise for this one, and I hope that many are blessed by the message that there is life after death. Heaven is real. It exists. I hope that perhaps "The Journey" may even bring a certain measure of comfort to those who have lost a loved one.

Yes, it is appointed unto man once to die. But rest assured that Jesus is the Way, the Truth, and the Life here on earth—and way beyond the grave. Christ has gone on to prepare a place for all of us who believe on His name.

When we get to that place, we will be known as we are known. We will know each other and rejoice forever in the light of the Lord when the final journey's made! Thank You, Lord!

Joe and Sabrina   *Photo courtesy of Joe Bonsall*

The Journey

I stumbled down a long dark road
From sunlight I had strayed
The demons came and beckoned me
I was lost and so afraid
I felt that I was falling
I thought it was a dream
I called upon my father
To come and rescue me

Oh father, rescue me

A door just seemed to open
The darkness turned to light
The Lord appeared before me
He wore a robe of white
He spoke my name so softly
I felt such peace within
He gently wrapped me in his arms
And forgave me all my sins

He forgave me all my sins

Another door was opened
A vision came so clear
I was on a ship now sailing
My Lord was standing near
He pointed towards the distant shore
And whispered to my soul
"Your journey now is o'er my child
Rejoice and welcome home"

Rejoice and welcome home

I saw my precious mother
She was waiting by the river
She smiled and waved and called my name
There were angels all around her
No sickness, pain, or sorrow,
No strife, no fear of war,
No devil's lies, no children cry,
All is peace forever more

There is peace forever more

Oh brother, my dear brother
Your life could end today
Except a man be born again
He cannot see the way
For Jesus there is waiting
To lead us past the grave
And take us home to be with him
When the final journey's made

When the final journey's made

THE SONG REMEMBERS

You have heard me say onstage and in print many times that songs mark time and space more so than just about any other barometer. We all remember moments in our lives when a song or songs were part of the experience. My mother cried whenever she heard "Sentimental Journey" because that was my parents' song.

Whenever I hear "Turn Your Eyes upon Jesus" I can see a fifteen-year-old Joey joining a few others around a campfire in Medford, New Jersey, accepting Jesus Christ as a real and personal Savior. A life-changing moment. A life-changing song!

Anyhow, I just experienced a glowing example of what I am writing about, and it appeared before me through the medium of a TV commercial, of all things.

A GE aircraft engine ad (which is silly in the first place because who among us is going to go out and buy one of those?) features the song "All I Need to Know." Mary and I both jumped.

Joe: "Oh man. I had not thought of that song in ages. I love that song. Remember? Linda Ronstadt and . . . and . . . ?"

Mary: "Umm, Neville Brother . . . big guy."

Joe: "Aaron Neville!"

Mary: "Yeah, him."

Joe: "Remember, we were driving in a rent-a-car from Reno to Lake Tahoe, and we heard it on the radio for the first time and I freaked!"

Mary: "Yeah, my crazy husband had to have it right now. You made several stops on the way until you found it."

Joe: "That was fun. I remember finding the CD at last at a Wal-Mart, and we cranked that song up loud all the way up the mountain. A great memory."

Mary: "I think that would have been a cassette, hon."

In our real heydays, playing Lake Tahoe at Harrah's Resort always provided a ton of good stories and great memories for Mary and me and all of the Oak Ridge Boys. So this morning, on this Fourth of July, while relaxing at home before taking on a day of cookouts and fireworks and counting blessings for the freedoms that we are enjoying as Americans—and Christians—one little song plays in an ad and opens a floodgate.

I would have never thought of the great little moment in time this morning if not for the song.

The song remembers . . .

Joe and Mary   *Photo courtesy of Joe Bonsall*

Sacrifice (For Me)

I wrote this song for the Oaks' Colors *project. The guys and producer Michael Sykes really liked it a lot, but the album was pretty full and there wasn't room for it. It took me six months to write this song, and I put my whole heart and soul into these lyrics. I think it is one of my better songs and will someday be recorded.*

Boy grew up in Caroline
Tobacco farm on the mountainside
Played football on the high school team
Fell in love with Sally Jean
He heard the call of Uncle Sam
Headed off to Viet Nam
When he comes home
Gonna settle down
But somewhere on the Mekong River
The soldier died
for me

Navajo boy stares at the sky
Bored with reservation life
He has hopes. He has dreams
Joins the United States Marines
A Marine works hard, he pulls his weight
His people are proud. He's a hero they say
When he comes home, it will be a new day
But somewhere in the desert
The Marine died
for me

(chorus)

So I can live
In the Land of Free
Raise my kids
Live my dreams
There's a price
For liberty
Sacrifice
for me

He punches that clock about half past eight
Just like any other day
Brooklyn fireman calling home
Gonna be late, something big's going on
The world had changed in just one day
The devil himself had sent those planes
When he gets home, gonna hold his wife
But somewhere in the tower
The fireman died
for me

(repeat chorus)

(reprise)

Long black wall
Field of green
Valley of fire
Distant beach
Cross of white
A hero dies
Sacrifice
For me

Words and music by Joseph S. Bonsall.
Copyright © 2003 B's in the Trees Music (ASCAP).
Administered by Gaither Copyright Management.

UNCLE LUTHER'S STUFFIN'

It is a beautiful afternoon in April 2005, and I find myself deeply embedded in the recording studio of our dear friend Michael Sykes on famous Music Row in downtown Nashville, Tennessee. The dogwoods and redbuds are in full bloom, and the tulips, my favorite flower, are beginning to pop up everywhere. It is a bit surreal to be singing Christmas songs in early spring, but that is what I am doing.

Under the able direction of co-producer Sykes and our own Ace, Duane Allen, I am putting down a final lead vocal on a song called "Uncle Luther Made the Stuffin'." Hopefully, many folks will hear it when our Oak Ridge Boys bluegrass and acoustic-driven Christmas project is released in the fall by Spring Hill Music.

A new Christmas project with a new feel and direction will refresh our holiday repertoire and certainly add spirit and creativity to our 2005 Christmas tour as well as our Feed the Children television specials.

"Hanging my stocking on the mantelpiece," I sing over a driving fiddle and banjo-dominated track. I am having a blast. I just cannot believe that we are actually singing and recording "Uncle Luther"!

You have heard me say many times that every song represents a story of its own as well as providing a personal time capsule for the listener—and the artist. "Luther's Stuffin' " is no exception.

When you hear the hook line, "Momma cooked the turkey . . . Uncle Luther made the stuffin'," you will smile. It is a fun song. A party song. A family song! As always, there is a real story lurking behind the music and lyrics. Here we go.

When I was a very young man of eighteen years old, I was singing with a little gospel band out of Philly called the Faith Four. We weren't very good, but we sure had fun. And every time I hit the stage with that little group, I was placing another stone on the pile that would someday grow into whom I have become.

We were booked to sing at a movie theater in Mahanoy City, Pennsylvania, by the theater owner, Luther Holt. It seemed that Mr. Holt loved gospel music, and about once month he would invite a group to come and sing in his historic Victoria Theater, which had become a famous coal region landmark by the middle of the sixties. Every major and part-time gospel group in Pennsylvania would eventually make its way to the "Vic," as it was called.

Luther had three daughters, and tenor boy fell hard for the youngest, Barbara. She was pretty, and she even had her own car. We dated for several years before we married. Right after I joined the Oaks in 1973, Barbara and I had a daughter, Jennifer. We eventually divorced, which is another chapter of its own, but suffice it to say, Barb was and is a wonderful woman—and I have always deeply loved and admired her family. Especially her father, Luther.

He was always very good to me. A wonderful Christian man and Bible scholar who put God first in all things, he was also a real inventor and innovator who played a vital role in the early days of cable television. It all started in Pennsylvania, you know. And his little company in Frackville, called Holt Electronics, supplied all the early components for the pioneer days of cable.

The man also made some might' fine stuffin'!

The Holts were of German and Pennsylvania Dutch decent, and Momma Holt, Marion, was a wonderful cook. She cooked up a big dinner in the old-fashioned way. Great beans, corn, pot roasts, and such—and on a holiday like Christmas or Thanksgiving, the whole family would gather in their humble little home and feast like kings and queens. Yes, Marion cooked the turkey, but Luther Holt always made the stuffin'!

To this day, I am not certain how he did it. A secret recipe? Strange and unusual seasonings? A magic touch? Whatever it was, that sure was some mighty fine stuffin'. He would tell the children that he made it with his feet, and they would run screaming. A funny memory.

I first thought of Luther's stuffin' as a song idea in 1984 when the Oaks decided to record a second Christmas album for MCA. My "Santa's Song" on the first album was actually my first real attempt at songwriting. So with a new project in the works, I felt confidant that I could write another Christmas song or two that might be relevant. So I wrote three. I remember I used a little Casio keyboard while staying at Bally's Hotel in Las Vegas when I wrote "First Christmas Day," "It's Christmas Time Once Again," and my first version of "Uncle Luther Made the Stuffin'."

I made Luther an uncle and tried to recreate the family reunion atmosphere that every family longs to have. Lots of relatives, lots of food, and a real memorable time. The kind of memories that stick to your soul.

Well, the group loved the first two songs, but the stuffin' song did not make it to the Oak Ridge Boys *Christmas Again* album in 1984. Years later we found ourselves on Capitol Records for about twenty-six minutes. We recorded a wonderful Christmas project for them, produced by Richard Landis. I wrote a song called "Daddy's Christmas Eve" for that project, which is a song that has meant a lot to me over the years.

I also decided to rewrite "Uncle Luther" as a rap song. Hey, it was the nineties, and I thought it was a fun idea! With the help of some good friends, we cut a heavy rap demo and pitched it to the Boys! Actually, everyone got a real kick out of it, but once again "Uncle Luther" was put aside. There was no way the Oaks were going to cut a rap song about stuffin'!

I mentioned "Uncle Luther" again in passing a few years ago, however, as you may recall, the stuffin' song did not appear on the *An Inconvenient Christmas* CD either.

I had all but given up on what I considered to be a fun song idea when, as fate would have it, a new opportunity presented itself with a Christmas project for 2005. Much like our *Journey* CD, this project would have a bluegrass acoustic feel.

One day a few months back we were on the bus getting ready for a show, and Duane Allen said to me, "You know man, that old 'Uncle Cracker' song of yours might fit this project. I never loved it, especially that awful rap version, however, you know me . . . when you can still remember a song after all these years, there must be something to it. You should rework it and bring it out again."

Then it hit me. "Uncle Luther" could be rewritten with a bluegrass feel. I was clicking my heels! I reached for the old banjer and went to work.

I rewrote the bridge and reformatted the verses a bit. I even wrote a new verse. I ran my early ideas of the new "grassy" version by Michael Sykes one day, and he just loved it. I was encouraged.

Then, the Mighty Oaks Band and I cut a kickin' demo of the song, and all of the Boys took to it. Yes!!

How about them apples? "Uncle Luther" was recorded by the Oak Ridge Boys twenty-one years after I wrote the first version!

My inspiration for the song, Jennifer's "Pap Pap" Luther Holt, is still alive today, although he is struggling with his health and needs your prayers. He is a good man, and I pity anyone who doesn't have someone like him in their family. Someday he will reunite with Marion in Glory. This is for certain!

I hope this fun little song causes everyone to reflect upon something wonderful in his or her Christmas past or present. Perhaps a good old family reunion with everyone there. Aunts and uncles, cousins and kids all over the place. A home that is alive with laughter and love— and great smells drifting in from the kitchen.

Back when Momma cooked the turkey . . . and Uncle Luther made the stuffin'!

Addendum

Luther Holt went home to be with Jesus on July 31, 2005. He has been reunited with his wife Marion and his oldest daughter, Joan. I am certain that, although this great man will be missed by those left behind, there is rejoicing in Glory at his Homecoming. We will see him again. I dedicate this fun little song to his memory!

Uncle Luther Made the Stuffin'

Cousin Lillie's hanging stockings on the mantelpiece
Daddy's puttin' tinsel on the Christmas tree
Granny's cuttin' cookies, pies a bakin' in the oven
Mamma cooked the turkey, Uncle Luther made the stuffin'

Brother David and the neighbors are a'shoveling snow
Little Vickie's wrapping presents with pretty red bows
Grandpa's makin' eggnog, the popcorn is a puffin'
Mamma cooked the turkey, Uncle Luther made the stuffin'

Artie from the army's comin' home tonight
Crazy Uncle Eddie's stringin' up the lights
Sister Sarah and her boyfriend are a kissin' and a huggin'
Mamma cooked the turkey, Uncle Luther made the stuffin'

Daddy's sittin' in his favorite chair
Trying to lead the family in a word of prayer
Jenny in the kitchen, sneakin' and a munchin'
Mamma cooked the turkey, Uncle Luther made the stuffin'

Aunt Anna's on piano, playin' Christmas songs
Tryin' hard to get the family just to sing along
The children all believin' that Santa is a'comin'
Mamma cooked the turkey, Uncle Luther made the stuffin'

(bridge)

Well the times they are a changin'
And the people keep a'movin'
I never will forget those
Happy family reunions
The kids are grown, the old folks gone
Christmas time was really something
When Mamma cooked the turkey, Uncle Luther made
    the stuffin'
Mamma cooked the turkey, Uncle Luther made the stuffin'

45

UNCLE LUTHER'S STUFFIN'

1 stick of margarine
1 large onion, chopped
3 cups of chopped celery
3 eggs, lightly beaten
Hot broth from the cooked turkey
3 six-ounce packages of seasoned crouton mix

While the turkey is baking, prepare the onion and celery. About ten minutes prior to the turkey coming out of the oven, place the margarine in a large cast iron skillet and melt it over low heat. Add the chopped onion and celery; turn the heat up to medium, and sauté the vegetables until they are soft but not browned. In the meantime, place the croutons in a large mixing bowl. Add the eggs and the sautéed vegetables.

Take the turkey out of the oven when done, and carefully pour the broth out of the turkey pan into the mixing bowl. Mix well. Use enough broth to moisten the mixture; however, the mixture should not be soggy. If you don't have enough broth from the turkey, you may substitute canned chicken broth, as needed.

Pour the mixture into the cast iron skillet. Adjust the oven to 350° and bake, uncovered, about 30 minutes or until browned. While the stuffin' is baking, the turkey will cool enough to be carved.

Daddy's Christmas Eve

Staring at the Christmas tree, I guess I couldn't sleep
The pretty lights hypnotize me, and I begin to think
It seems like only yesterday that I was just a boy
Dreaming of the reindeer sleigh and Santa's bag of toys

A lot of years have slipped by, a lot of things have changed
But the magic of this special night somehow remains the same
I'm so thankful for my little ones, oh how I love them so
I know, God, how you must have felt on that Christmas long
ago

You must have cried a million tears on that first Christmas Eve
You knew your one and only Son would someday die for me
Staring out my window, I can see the Christmas star
It seems a little brighter now than it had before

Help me be the kind of dad that you would have me be
I guess I'll go on up to bed, thank you, Lord, for Christmas Eve
I guess I'll go on up to bed, thank you, Lord, for Christmas Eve

Words and music by Joseph S. Bonsall.
Copyright © 1994 B's in the Trees Music (ASCAP).
Administered by Gaither Copyright Management.

MUSIC—MY PERSPECTIVE

I have loved music for as long as I can remember. In fact the music business has been the focal point of my entire adult life. That would be performance, recording, management, production, logistics, marketing, promotion, touring, and publishing—and even a bit of songwriting from time to time. I have spent my years surrounded by singers and musicians and songwriters, most of whom possessed more talent than me. And I have been blessed with the fact that I am always learning from them.

As a singer, I have known the best! Singing next to Duane Allen on stage for over thirty-seven years has been more of a constant study in how to sing than anything I could have ever learned in any other forum.

As a banjo student, I have the opportunity to study many great musicians and see how they apply and hone their craft over time. I am thankful for the opportunity to glean and to share in that knowledge.

The Mighty Oaks Band is the most respected group of players in the business. They are all great guys and, man, they can play! I have learned much from each of them.

Living in Nashville, one comes in constant contact with the finest songwriters in the world. It is impossible not to pick up a hint or two or three as to how to construct a song or how a song should be constructed.

The plain and simple bottom line here, though, is that I sing songs for a living, and it has been a wondrous and incredible journey to be sure. I thank God for this career every single day.

As a fan, my taste in music is very eclectic. My iPod is full of variety, and the genres of the stuff I listen to stretches and blurs the lines between rock and country and bluegrass and classical. Not sure how to categorize Frank Sinatra, Dean Martin, and Johnny Mathis, but I assure you they are there. I never have liked labels though. To me it is good or it is not good. You either like it or you do not. The bottom line is the song, and I am about to elaborate.

Whether I am listening to Bruce Springsteen, Andrea Bocelli, the Grascals, or the Gaither Vocal Band, for that matter, I am always looking for the great song. Carrie Underwood singing "Jesus Take the Wheel." Brad Paisley and Dolly Parton singing "When I Get Where I Am Going." Brooks and Dunn singing "I Believe." Vince Gill singing "Go Rest High on that Mountain" or Janet Paschal singing "Another Soldier Has Come Home." Bob Seger singing, well, almost anything. But you get the picture.

As the aforementioned longtime lead voice of the Oak Ridge Boys, Duane Allen would say, "It is the song that matters." He calls it three minutes of magic and, thankfully, we have had our share of great songs to sing over all these years.

I find myself always looking for a great song to listen to. Sometimes I will scan across the radio dial, saying, "Come on, someone play me a great song! Please!" I am sure many of us do just that and, quite honestly, sometimes one will wade through a ton of mediocrity before landing on that piece of magic.

Whether it is a big hit or a demo by an obscure writer or perhaps an album cut that jumps out and grabs you right by the heart, it is the song! It is the song! At least that should be the case. Just think about it—a great singer singing a great song? What a concept!

I am fond of saying that all music was once new, and that is a truism. Duane would answer that it is only the great songs that stand the test of time, and we are both correct in the analysis. Every song was indeed once new but not necessarily worth keeping on the playlist.

Can you say "My Way" by the Chairman? Or "The Pretender" by Jackson Browne? How about "In Color" by Jamey Johnson, or "Thank God for Kids" by William Lee Golden and the Oak Ridge Boys? I could go on.

I do not know much about the urban hip-hop kind of music that is played today, except to say that is perhaps the only genre I find distasteful, and not because I am a white boy. Rather that I just cannot find the song in the midst of it all. It is all beat and rhythmic poetry of sorts that does not apply to my life, so I guess I block it out. I do, however, love rhythm and blues. Give me Gladys Knight or the Stylistics any day to Lil Wayne or Eminem. Remember "Midnight Train to Georgia"? Woo hoo! I just recently heard Smokey Robinson sing live for the first time in my sixty-two years on the planet, and I was stunned into submission by that sweet voice and stage presence.

It is, perhaps, relevant that I never cared much for disco music either, but I did and always have loved the Bee Gees. The vocal thing is probably the reason, however, they also have recorded some great songs, before and after disco when they were "Jive Talking" us to death. I also "Love that Old Time Rock and Roll. That Sort of Music just Soothes My Soul!" Smiles . . .

I have written much about Elvis, but I also loved many of the other early acts of that day like, for example, Ricky Nelson. I have a lot of Ricky on my iPod. "Hello Mary Lou, Goodbye Heart!"

The doo-wop groups of the late fifties and early sixties are also very meaningful to iPod boy. Danny and the Juniors' "At the Hop" still works for me.

The big admission: I did not like the British Invasion of 1964. I did not even like the Beatles, although my respect for them has grown over time. I just thought that acts like the Dave Clark Five, Herman's Hermits, and the Rolling Stones were ushering in a big change, and I was not happy with it. Hey, I was in high school. I was chasing girls. I was trying to find myself. I thought it was the end of my kind of rock and roll, and you know what? It was!

The British groups set the table for the late sixties, free love and hippie flower power, protest songs, much of which had an almost evil edge. The war in Vietnam, the ugly race riots, and the drug culture had a lot to do with that, of course. And eventually the Eagles would save us all from "The Eve of Destruction," when they laid it all back and told us to "Take It Easy." But for me? I turned my attention to gospel quartets and Merle Haggard, and I am happy to say I still listen to them today.

My favorite gospel groups have changed a bit from the old Statesmen, Blackwood Brothers, and Cathedral Quartet to Ernie Haas and Signature Sound, the Gaithers, and the Isaacs. And as far as traditional country is concerned, I am happy that Merle Haggard is still around. God bless him!

As a banjo player, I listen to a ton of bluegrass music as well, and I love all of the big acts because they all can really pick it. As they say, a bad musician cannot hide in top-tier bluegrass. If I grabbed my banjo and sat in with Cherryholmes or Dailey and Vincent or Ricky Skaggs and Kentucky Thunder, someone just might open fire.

But as a professional singer I constantly find myself navigating from gospel to country, while I still possess an old rocker's heart and energy and attitude. I guess I have made a pretty good living by riding upon that rail for a long time now. It is this kind of open mindedness and being willing to stretch the musical boundaries that has kept the Oak Ridge Boys alive for decades, and I pray that God will let it all last as long as possible.

Four different men with four different backgrounds stand on that stage every night and make magic happen for those who might be dwelling in our circumference of being at that given moment, and it is a joyful thing to be a part of. I learn something from my singing partners, Duane Allen, William Lee Golden, and Richard Sterban, every single day.

There is a right way and there is a "no way." I thank God daily for placing me with a group of men who are always forward thinking, yet possess a firm hold on the traditions of who and what we are. We are not the young guys anymore, but we are still out here singing to a lot of people year after year. We are so very are thankful to God above for the good health and for the ability to still be grinding it out on the never-ending tour. We give Him the honor, praise, and glory for all of these blessings.

I have never taken the music for granted. To me it is a daily gift, and I do not believe that I could ever exist without it. A great producer once told me that if you take care of the music, then the music will take care of you. I have done my best to take care of the music. But I assure you that I could never give back enough to makeup for the constant joy that it has given to me over my entire life. Music has been my entire life.

Somebody play a good song!

LIFE

STONES

I have spent my adult life on the road. I left the Jack Frost Sugar Company in Philadelphia when I was nineteen years old to join up with my singing brother Richard Sterban and begin singing full-time with the gospel group known as the Keystone Quartet. I had been singing part-time with my own little Faith Four group before that, and, of course, Richard and I have now been singing with the Oak Ridge Boys since the early seventies.

I was just twenty-five years old when I joined Duane Allen, William Lee Golden, and my old friend Richard, and we embarked on this amazing and blessed musical journey. I am now well over sixty, and I still find myself boarding the bus with my best friends and singing songs across America and beyond.

Talk about having a hand in the cookie jar. I have spent my entire life singing songs for a living. I have had a microphone in my hand since the time I was a young boy who could only dream about the day that I might find myself singing on the big stage and riding on a tour bus, surrounded with men of like minds—and like dreams.

All of this happened, and I thank God each day for the pathways that He has allowed me to walk upon and for the experiences and blessings He has bestowed upon me personally. I feel blessed way beyond any deserving.

I really believe that every life is a mountain. We spend our whole journey placing little stones in a pile that eventually becomes that mountain. It takes years to build, yet the journey is really a short one within the big picture. The book of James tells us that our lives are but a vapor that passes quickly, and I must admit my vapor appears to be moving right on along.

The Bible also says that it is only what is done for Christ that will last, so I guess some stones do not mean as much as others. Yet I still believe that each stone placed is indeed relevant to what and whom we are and what we are becoming as the years fly on by. Each story, each verse, each memory, each song, each fork in the road, and each person who has ever influenced us are all very meaningful.

Each of us is blessed in so many ways because from the time we were little God would begin to speak to us in that sweet and still, small voice. The advice has always been there. His guidance and healing have always been just a prayer away. The love of Jesus is always just a breath away.

The door has always been open and the music has been playing. It is such a shame that so many are just not listening. You will read over and over in my writings and musings about the importance of listening. One must keep their ears and heart and mind open to the constant blessings that God provides to us all. They are there every moment of every day. However, most of us are so dead set in our individual pursuit of happiness, money, and success that we miss many of these things.

We worry when we need not worry. We fear when we need not to be fearful. The fast-paced life that we lead tends to close us in. Our hearts often harden with the burden of self-centered narcissism that drowns out that still, small voice that pleads with us to slow it on down and be silent for a bit.

I always believed that I would sing. I have always loved to sing, and my mother, Lillie, always encouraged me to do just that. Small Stone: My mom and my dad would have a couple of folks over for canasta, a game I have never figured out how to play. Invariably, I would be asked to sing for these neighbors, most of whom were war veterans like my parents, who all smoked Winston cigarettes and drank a fair share of Ballantine beer. Well, all but Lillie, of course, who always taught me that drinking and smoking will "kill ya dead!"

But sing for them I would, gospel songs my mom taught me and maybe a little Sinatra or Dean Martin. Standing in that little room and belting one out was always fun for me. Not just because I was a little hambone, but I loved to see my mother smile. I am thankful I had a mother who smiled at me and was proud of me and loved me with all her heart. Lillie provided most of the early stones for little Joey Bonsall.

I would sing whenever she asked me to sing and always give it all I had inside me to give. I would also sing in church all alone on the stage of the Calvary Church of the Brethren, singing "Gloryland Way" or "Dust on the Bible." Each performance became a little stone on the mountain. Each song would prepare for me for a lifetime of songs.

Stone: My mom enters me into a contest on Philadelphia's WCAU, Channel 10, Horn and Hardart Talent Scouts show at the age of four. I sang "If They Made Me a King" on Saturday morning television. I did not win, and the memory is a little smoky although nowhere near forgotten.

Stone: Some church kids led by George Weber and a neighbor named Bunky Smulling, who was a little older and drove a 1960 white Buick convertible with a red interior, invited me to go to a Southern gospel music concert in Ardmore, Pennsylvania. They said if I did not like it they would never bother me again. I went with them and fell in love with quartet music.

That night I saw the Blackwood Brothers with J. D. Sumner singing bass and the Couriers out of Harrisburg, Pennsylvania. Those kids took me off the streets and put me on a pathway to a life of music. Those same kids also lead me to the Lord at age fifteen. That Buick turned out to be one huge stone—perhaps the only car to ever lead a kid to Christ.

Stone: I wrote a letter to J. D. Sumner, of the Blackwood Brothers at that time and told him about my desire to sing in a group one day. He answered back and told me to let nothing get in the way of my dreams. In later years we would become friends. I would even buy a tour bus from him and allow him to beat me at the game of chess. Right!

Stone: I talked my dad into taking me to a big gospel concert in Harrisburg in 1963. That town was about 100 miles from Philly. It might as well have been the moon as far as he was concerned, but miracle of miracles, he took me.

When we entered the backdoor of the Farm Show Arena, the group on stage was the original Keystone Quartet. As we made our way to our seats, their nineteen-year-old bass singer, Richard Sterban, was soloing on "Let the Lower Lights Be Burning." I said hello to him that night and shook his hand. I met another young man by the name of Ronnie Graeff that night. He was my age and seemed to love the music as much as I did. I found out that Ron only lived about twelve blocks from where I lived in Philly and that he was in a little group called the Faith Four and was looking for another singer. How many years did I sing in the Faith Four, and then the Keystones? Quite a few!

Stone: After playing Pop Warner league football, I figured that making the high school team would be a snap. After all I was a two-year all-star wide receiver in the 125 pound division. It was not a snap. I nearly got myself killed! So I joined the famous Frankford High School Ambassadors of Song, under the direction of Robert G. Hamilton. This was a man who would inspire me and help to guide my life. I toured Scandinavia with "Mr. H" and the choir. I have never forgotten him or that wonderful group of friends who shared the experience of a lifetime.

That trip alone was a huge stone on my mountain. It taught me at age fifteen how to prepare for a singing tour and how to get along with people and learn new things about other countries and cultures. As a side note, you must read *G.I. Joe and Lillie* to get a perspective of this time period in my life and how my mom made this trip happen for me.

How about writing?

Folks always ask if I ever wanted to write, and the honest answer would have been no. But thinking back, I can remember a little Joey writing made-up stories about a gunfighter named Providence Joe. And I can also remember making up superhero stories about two characters by the name of Big Fox and Little Fox. My sister Nancy and I acted out those characters inside our musty basement at 3517 Jasper Street. We even had wooden swords. (Could there ever be superhero fox with a sword? Guess so!)

I also used to write stories about the Philadelphia Phillies in longhand and on loose-leaf book paper. I even starred as the second baseman in some of those tall tales. I would love to have all of those writings now, but my mom probably threw them out with my baseball cards and marble collection around 1978—the only time I can ever remember really wanting to harm her!

I could go on and on and on from those stones that pertained to singing and writing and finding Jesus. How about those other stones that led up to meeting my Mary and raising two wonderful daughters, Jen and Sabrina? I imagine I could continue this little commentary forever, but I think by now you get the picture.

Each and every life is important, and each and every life is indeed a mountain made up of little stones that are put in place over the passing years. The Bible teaches us that we are all very important and that God knows us and cares about us and loves us. The Bible also says every single hair on our head is numbered by the same God who also knows when each sparrow falls. Are we not more important than the sparrow?

Jesus would indicate that we are!

So slow it all down just a little, and open up your ears and your heart and your mind as to what God's plan is for your life. Take the time to listen! It is imperative to do so. God will provide the guidance, and He will put the right people at different crossroads of your life, people who will help you make the right decisions along your journey.

Remember, each little stone becomes the mountain that is you. Be humble and prayerful as you build so as to become someone who is a blessing to people. Accept Christ into your heart and allow Him to lead, guide, and direct, and if you do that your mountain will be strong and your eternity will be in Glory, as is His promise.

So here I am. Joseph, Joe, Joey, Ban-Joey, Daddy, Pop Pop, and "Honey, will you *please* change that light-bulb over the garage!" and we all seem to be just fine. I sing, I write, I work on my farm, I love my family, and I pick a little banjo.

I have become a mountain of God's mercies and blessings, and I am so very thankful. However, this journey is not yet over. If it be God's will, then many more stones will be added over the coming years.

For me this very book is a huge stone. Thanks for sharing it with me, and may God bless and guide you all on your journey here, all the while preparing you for the new journey that lies ahead.

OUR MOLLY

"**M**olly was two years old but still looked somewhat like a kitten. It is just that she never grew very big."

This was the opening line of my Molly the Cat book series published by Ideals Children's Books in the early nineties. There were four books in the series, and writing about Molly and her friends provided me with the joys of getting close to children again.

It would still be a while before my grandchildren would be born. My daughters had long grown, and all of a sudden, thanks to Molly, I was speaking to third- and fourth-grade children on a weekly basis about writing, positive thinking, and dreaming and imagination, and . . . cats. What if cats could think and talk in their own language? What would be going on in their world? Fun stuff!

Just like in the first Molly book, my nephew Gabriel actually did gather up a soaking wet little calico kitten he had found under a tree and brought her home to Mary and me. We already had three cats at the time, a big orange Tabby named Pumpkin, another stray who happened by the name of Gypsy, and a cute little boy named Omaha, who we found in a pet store in Omaha, Nebraska. We had just lost a little Russian Blue boy named Yuri. He passed away much too soon due to kidney disease, so our hearts were a bit heavy when this multicolored little kitten arrived. She fit right in and definitely brightened up the whole place.

"Well, good golly, Miss Molly," said Mary and the name stuck. It fit her perfectly. Molly was and still is a very beautiful little girl kitty.

If you ever read the books *Molly, The Home, Outside,* and *Brewster,* it is a point of interest that all the cats and the one dog, Brewster, who appeared in the series have all gone on to that Better Place provided for them by the God of All Creatures, except for our Molly.

Spooker, The Dude, Red, Gypsy, Pumpkin, and little Omaha, as well as the slobbering bulldog Brewster, were all based upon real life creatures who lived in and around "The Home," as I referred in the books to our house full of cats.

Molly is now sixteen years old and still looks somewhat like a kitten, and I believe she really does know she was a star for a while. My dream was to see her on the big screen someday and, who knows, it could still happen.

Molly now shares the home with a different bunch of kitties: Sally Ann, Ted, Baybe', Callie, Sunny, and a new kitten named Crockett, who, as fate would have it, was found by our nephew Gabriel. He just seems to have a knack for this sort of thing. We also have two outdoor kitties named Blackie and LT, who choose to live with us as well.

As Mark Twain once said, "Having cats leads to having more cats!" They sure seem to know where the love and the food are, not necessarily in that order.

Right now, our kitten Crockett is the center of our cat universe. He is a very funny little fellow and just beautiful. He is champagne and white tiger kitty, and he is quite stunning, as well as being lots of fun.

Perhaps a new series of books on Crockett is in order for the next year or so. He is a character, and the other kitties would make great cohorts for him in a new series. I could make Molly the old Sage, as I did for Pumpkin in the first set of books. Indeed, my creative wheels are turning here, and I can already hear the catspeak in my head, as Crockett gets in and out of one jam after another.

But back to Molly.

She is the one who is responsible for Mary and me starting the Joseph S. and Mary Ann Bonsall Foundation that raises money, and then distributes it to humane centers around the country. Thanks to the Molly books, many a cat or dog has found a good home. We have helped children's literacy causes and pet education projects as well, thanks to our little calico kitty and the impact she has had on our lives.

Molly is a bit stiff and she moves much slower these days. She does not jump as high or run as fast. She is content to stay in one room most of the time and watch Animal Planet on television. I kid you not. It is always on for her. She loves her bed, which is under a desk, but when she hears different sounds on TV, especially monkey sounds, she gets out of her bed and jumps up on her chair and watches the show for hours. I have witnesses!

She loves our other big calico, Callie (another stray who ended up in the care of Mother Mary), but really does not have much time or patience these days for the others. She is the old girl now, and she can pretty much do as she wants. In my heart she will always be our star.

The point of this little piece of writing is simple. Animals have so much to teach us, and responsible pet ownership is very important. Some think that cats and dogs are throwaway objects, disposable elements in our life, but Mary and I urge you to think differently about these precious pets God has allowed into our lives. They need care and love just as humans do, and if God knows when a sparrow falls, he knows when a dog or a kitty is abused or ignored. If you cannot handle pet ownership, then quite simply do not adopt one. But if your heart is willing and committed to a new friend who would share your space, then by all means do not miss the opportunity.

Mary and I love all our cats very much. They are each different one from the other and their blend of independence, agility, humor, and companionship has been a blessing to our home.

So, from Mother Mary and me as well as Crockett, Sunny, Blackie, LT, The Baybe, Sally Ann, Callie, Ted and our Molly, may the God of All Creatures continue to bless you and yours!

Addendum

I would like to dedicate this little story to Bud, our gray and white kitty who passed on to the Better Place a short time ago. He came to our house to live one day and a funny thing happened. After about a year his owners came by the house and said, "'Monk has chosen to live with you and not with us any longer, so here are his papers." They left in tears! Well, Mary had been calling him Bud, so that is what we named him. He was a wonderful friend. He guarded the perimeter, and we even let him in when he wanted inside. He would climb the screen doors when he wanted in. He developed an enlarged heart and all of a sudden he was gone. We loved our Bubba!!!

For more information on the Joseph S. and Mary Ann Bonsall Foundation, visit http://www.josephsbonsall.com.

A CUP LA DAZE

On Monday, June 23, 2002, at approximately 9:30 a.m. Eastern time, I found myself standing beside my parents' graves in Arlington National Cemetery. I had flown into D.C. early that morning to tape a segment with Brit Hume for a Fox News Network Fourth of July program.

I have to admit I was more than a bit tired. The Oak Ridge Boys had been hitting the road hard the last few weeks, including a performance on the Grand Ol' Opry in Nashville the previous Saturday night.

We had been away from home for most of June. From the Windmill Festival in Nebraska to the RV Fest in Louisville, on through Arkansas with stops in Missouri, Ohio, Michigan, Alabama, Virginia, and Pennsylvania—we had been doing a lot of singing on the summer portion of our Red, White, and BluBlocker Tour.

After the Opry I drove out to my farm and joined my wife for a day of work and good food. Needless to say, I went to bed late that Sunday and got up really early for my flight to Washington on Monday morning. Like we used to say in our younger days, "This going to bed at 5:45 a.m. and getting up at 6 a.m. is gonna kill us!"

So on that breezy and warm Monday morning, after placing a book on the grave of G.I. Joe and Lillie Bonsall, I headed for the Fox News studios, where just a few weeks earlier, the whole group had taped a show with Cal Thomas.

At that time, being the Fox News junkies that we are, the Boys literally invaded the place. No one was safe, not Brit Hume, not Tony Snow, or anyone else whose talking head we recognized from our satellite Channel 360!

We had a ball and handed out sufficient quantities of our *Colors* CDs and my *G.I. Joe and Lillie* books.

Well, it seems that Mr. Hume read my book and immediately invited me to come back to Fox to tape a segment he was putting together for his July Fourth show. After makeup, Brit Hume and I sat and chatted for a while about the show.

I wish the camera had been on for this intimate conversation. He told me that he loved my book and that it moved him deeply. He told me that the most moving experience in his many years of journalism was covering the fiftieth anniversary of D-Day in June 1994 from Normandy, France. His eyes grew moist as he spoke. I have always liked and respected this man, and as he candidly spoke to me in that dressing room on his sixtieth birthday, I came to like him even more.

We spoke about *G.I. Joe and Lillie* on the set for about eight minutes. He was so nice to me. He held my little book in his hands the whole time and facing the camera told the whole country that it was a good book. I was nervous and a bit emotional in the presence of this legendary journalist, and I wished that I had been a bit more rested. I think I could have spoken a little more eloquently.

By the way, that view of the Capitol building on his set really is a view of the Capitol building. It is not a fake TV picture!

On the way out, Brit Hume introduced me to Armstrong Williams, which was also a real honor. The Supreme Court had just handed down their controversial ruling on racial quotas for college entrance, and Mr. Armstrong was there at Fox News to lend a black conservative viewpoint. Brit Hume recommended that Mr. Armstrong read the book and listen to *Colors*. And I was right there to provide him with a copy of each! What an honor.

Good friends of Mary's and mine were kind enough to pick me up at the airport and hang out with me for the six hours or so that day. Ed White works for the Department of the Interior's Fish and Wildlife Division, and his wife Sandy worked in the Pentagon for years. After the taping the Whites dropped me back at the airport, where I would fly on to Norfolk to tape an appearance on the *700 Club* the following day.

I am pleased to report that there is a great sushi bar in the Reagan airport, and after getting my fill of tuna, yellowtail, salmon, and a few rainbow rolls, I boarded a small U.S. Airways prop job called a Dash 8 and flew to Norfolk.

That part of the trip was a nightmare! I was stuffed in the back and the plane was packed. It was also stifling. Why couldn't they cool this thing down? It was only a forty-minute flight to Norfolk, but for yours truly, a borderline claustrophobe, it seemed like six hours.

As we flew over Norfolk, Virginia, I looked down and saw several battleships and destroyers in the harbor. Then . . . my eye caught several old WWII landing craft. Big LCI's (Landing Craft Infantry). I choked up a little thinking how cramped up those guys were fifty-nine years earlier. My father could have been aboard one of those very ships as he crossed the channel. It made me feel a little better. Thankfully, we landed within five minutes.

Mr. Derrick Brown was holding a *700 Club* placard with my name on it when I deplaned. He took me to the Founders Inn in Virginia Beach, where I scurried to room 2201, turned the AC as low as it would go, took a hot shower, called Mary, crawled into bed, and slept for twelve hours!

The next day I awoke around 8 a.m. and ordered a huge breakfast on Pat Robertson! After all, I had pretty much slept through dinner.

The *700 Club* television studios, the Founders Inn, and a huge university are all part of this monstrous complex, and I was honored to be there.

After makeup, I had a production meeting with the CEO of the Christian Broadcasting Network, Mr. Little, and an extraordinary group of women led by Molly Young. We spoke for a while about the future of country music television since TNN was gone. CBN had some great ideas for new programming that would originate from a new complex on Dickerson Road in Nashville. The network had recently purchased this facility from Qwest Communications. Mr. Little asked if I might be interested in being a part of this project as a possible host, and I told him that I would talk about it again later when I wasn't so busy. *That might be in 2015!* His ideas were sound, though, and some new country music programming would be welcome.

The aforementioned *700 Club* show was really special. Airing on July Fourth, it featured a wonderful Christian photographer from Australia, who had spent three years lugging a camera across America; an endearing little Christian man from New York, who had been in charge of maintaining the Statue of Liberty for thirty years; and . . . your author.

Before the taping, Dr. Robertson and I reflected back to the Republican National Convention in New Orleans in 1988, when the Oak Ridge Boys and the Republican nominee George Herbert Walker Bush shared the stage as balloons and confetti fell on our heads. Pat Robertson had made a good run at the nomination that year, and he was up there with us supporting Bush. I could tell that he was enjoying the chance to reflect on that night and obviously remembered it well.

Before the cameras rolled I thanked him for the positive influence he had been on American politics during the last several years. He was responsible for energizing many Christians to get out to the polls and vote for candidates who reflect American values and godly ideals. Dr. Pat Robertson is a good and special man.

After showing Oaks footage, he held up my book and encouraged his audience to buy and read *G.I. Joe and Lillie*. It was a wonderful interview, and I am grateful to him for the incredible way he treated me, the Oaks, and my book.

After the taping, I was led by Molly Hunt to the chapel, where about 200 employees of the CBN organization were in prayer for our nation and leaders. It was very moving. Mr. Little introduced me as the day's speaker, and I took the floor.

I spoke lightly at first. I did my routine about how my middle name is "Of The," as in "Aren't you one of the . . . ? There goes one of the . . . " and so on.

I had them all laughing. After bringing regards from all the Boys, I talked for a while about how fortunate I was to be living out my dreams in this great land and about how fortunate I am to be with the Oak Ridge Boys, a group of men who try their best every day to live right, honor God and affect people in a positive way.

I spoke about my "Crossroads Theory" and how God places different people in our pathway to help us make the right turns. I gave a few personal examples and encouraged them to always keep their hearts and minds open to God's call and plan for their lives.

I closed by talking about the two most important people I ever met at life's crossroads: my mother and Jesus Christ. The place stood as one and applauded.

Then some guy yelled out, "Sing 'Elvira'!"

Everyone laughed. He yelled again. "Sing anything," and they kept applauding. So I sang "G.I. Joe and Lillie" acappella. It was very cool.

I flew to Nashville through Charlotte, North Carolina (Mom's home state), and arrived at the house around 8 p.m. My Mary had dinner waiting. I told her all about the last "cup la daze," repacked, and climbed aboard the bus for Branson.

The Big Apple

After two great shows in Branson at the Grand Palace, we awoke on the bus just outside the airport in St. Louis and boarded a plane ultimately headed toward the Big Apple.

We landed in Pittsburgh, Pennsylvania, and spent about an hour eating sushi inside a mall there. The Oaks and our road manager, Captain Irish (Timmer Ground) all chowing down on tuna and eel rolls was a sight that could possibly indicate that the apocalypse is truly upon us. What have I created?

We landed in New York City and were met by Spring Hill Music publicist Beth Blinn, who had secured for us a spot on *Hannity and Colmes,* and it was great to have her with us. We checked into the Edison hotel, which took forever. Around 7:30 p.m. we met downstairs in the lobby and headed for Fox News, where we immediately established a beachhead and attacked with abandon.

We pre-taped our interview with Sean Hannity and Alan Colmes at 8:15 p.m. for broadcast on Friday, June, 27, and it all went very well. Sean was just wonderful—and so was Alan. They treated us like gold, and we had a ball.

Sean Hannity loved *Colors*! He said he would play it on his radio show because "America needs to hear songs like this." Sean is heard on numerous stations, and his support of Daryl Worley's "Do You Remember" song is what started the groundswell and made it a huge hit. We knew that Sean Hannity was a great guy, and he didn't let us down a bit.

Our old friend Jack Kemp, now with Empower America, was there, as was one of our Fox favorites, Shepard Smith. We all gathered in a semicircle and talked for about thirty minutes. Right in front of everyone Jack thanked us "for representing what is right about this great country of ours." It was very moving. Beth Blinn gave copies of *Colors* and *G.I. Joe and Lillie* to everyone and took pictures!

Then we sat in the studio for the live *Hannity and Colmes* broadcast. It was a busy news day with the Supreme Court, once again, handing down a controversial decision, this one involving gay sex. In another court, the verdict was reached for the Texas woman involved in the windshield murder. We left the Fox studios with a standing invitation to come back anytime to do *Hannity and Colmes,* as well as an invite to do *Fox and Friends* and Sean's radio show.

I went back to my room, changed clothes, and walked around Times Square for a while. At 11 p.m. the streets were packed. There is an amazing energy that permeates these streets. With huge video billboards everywhere, it reminded me just a little bit of the movie *Blade Runner* with Harrison Ford. I think I saw a Replicant or two walking around just outside the Matrix.

The musical *Urinetown* was just letting out as I passed the theater right off Broadway. *Urinetown!!!* What? The theater had been packed too! Only in New York, I guess.

I walked a few more blocks and found a little Italian restaurant called Tony DiNapolis. Hey, Tony and Carmella had eaten there and so had Paulie Walnuts, so it had to be good. In fact, Michael Corleone may have shot Salottzo in this very establishment.

I ordered veal piccatta and linguine with garlic and olive oil, sipped on some good cab and thought of home. My Mary had probably been in bed for two hours and was no doubt fast asleep—with at least three kitties resting against or on top of her. And here I sat by myself, eating pasta at a corner table nestled in the middle of the most energetic city in the world. I had just taped *Hannity and Colmes,* but I missed my wife . . . and the kitties . . . and home.

Oh well, I'll be there in just a cup la daze!

BARNEY

It was a beautiful day on the farm. I was all caught up on my yard mowing and weed eating. Therefore, I figured I would take an opportunity to hop aboard my big John Deere 5410 and drag my ten-foot rotary cutter over to the back pasture and knock down weeds.

The farm is a beehive of activity as several good neighbors are happily cutting, raking, and baling hay from many of my fields. I get a clean pasture and they get hundreds of rolls of hay for their winter cattle feed. There are five tractors here right now, all hard at work.

These events always take place in the early summer and fall, and I usually end up only bushhogging whatever fields my neighbor, Harold Pitcock, and his men avoid. My back pasture is usually pretty weedy, so I always get to cut that field. Only the best grass is rolled up for future consumption. Moo!

I greased up all the lube points on the rotary cutter, cranked up the engine on the big green JD, and let her warm up a bit. It is mid-July, in the summer heat, and humidity is hanging so thick in the air you can actually see it.

I back out of the barn and start heading up the drive toward the house and beyond, when to my surprise I notice a baby barn swallow precariously perched on a hydraulic hose at the top of the front loader. He is weaving back and forth and does not fly off, despite the loud noise and vibration.

I pull over by the house, and my wife Mary comes running from the front porch. I call her eagle-eye because, although her eyesight is not the best (she has worn glasses since early childhood), the woman can pick up a piece of dirt on the living room carpet from any vantage point inside the county. Especially if it came in on my shoe!

Mary had indeed noticed the little swallow on the tractor from the time I came out of the barn, which is a good sixty yards from the house. I shut off the big diesel engine and climbed down from the royal yellow seat. Both of us gazed up at the very scared and seemingly very disoriented little bird.

Here in the holler that lies on the Monroe, Kentucky-Macon County, Tennessee, line, barn swallows are part of the landscape. At the end of March one pair usually shows up first. They remind me of wagon-train scouts checking out the lay of the land. "Yep, this here is the place. All seems well. Fly back and tell the others to come on down! There are lots of places to nest and plenty of flying bugs to eat. It's going to be a great summer."

All of a sudden there are six barn swallows, and soon ten or twelve. By early April, there are twenty or thirty making nests in the eaves of the house and in the lean-tos and—are you ready?—*the barns!*

We can lie in our bedroom and look out the window and see at least three nests close up. We have studied these magical little birds for years, and it is always a blessing to be able to watch them fly, eat, mate, lay eggs, and hatch babies, then to watch them grow and eventually leave the nest. The process begins again, all summer long over and over until September, when there are well over two hundred barn swallows living here, with Mary and me as their guests.

There are two electrical wires that run from a pole in the yard to the house. (We are the last ones served on the Tri County Co-op line.) Each night throughout the season, just before the birds are ready to assault mosquitoes for their evening meal, they tend to line up on the wires, making it easy for me to count them.

I want to interject some vital info at this point, for the birders amongst my readers. *Hirundo Rustica* is the Latin name for the barn swallow. Every species actually has a name like this, although we never use them in our daily conversation. I am actually *Homo Sapien Erectus Banjoist,* while my wife is *Femalia Sapien Stop and Pick Up Some Milkus*!

Barn swallows can be found throughout much of the world and are resident on all continents except Australia. This species is easily distinguished from other swallows, like the rough winged swallow or the cave swallow, by its distinctively forked tail and its rust-colored under parts.

The barn swallow's aerial maneuvering is like no other bird. It can effortlessly make sharp turns while flying at high speed, which makes it easy for the bird to gobble up large volumes of flying insects. They remind me of little stealth fighter jets.

When feeding young, the swallows will fly from before dawn until after sunset. They seem to know just when to take a little rest and then go at it again. They nest in colonies, and they are, quite frankly, the most communicative birds I have ever seen. They seem to have a unique language, and they will often chat with one another using various chirps. They have a dolphin-like sound going when they want to make a point. It is downright amazing.

They fly together and hunt together and protect their environs as one. If a predator approaches a nest, many birds will gang up, attack, and harass the enemy until it runs off.

Swallows love to co-exist with the farmer because human activity seems to stir up insects. Sometimes forty or fifty birds will descend upon a tractor at work, all the while swooping and diving and collecting food. There have been times when I just knew I was going to get knocked off the machine or at least take a good peck in the head. But it has never happened.

These birds also mate for life, and the love a swallow shares with its mate is a wonderful thing to behold. I once saw a series of pictures on the Internet of a female barn swallow that had been hit by a car. As she lay there near to death, the male brought her food and stood watch over her for hours. When she passed, he actually screamed out in sorrow.

But back to Barney. *Of course* I named him Barney! He would not fly from the tractor, so I gently placed my index finger under his belly just above his feet, as you would a pet parakeet, and he climbed aboard.

How very sweet he was. I had, unfortunately, seen many of these little guys that did not make it to full-fledged adulthood. I have seen them fall out of nests and break their necks. I have seen their remains after a lost battle with a snake. On a rare occasion I have actually seen little ones like Barney fall right out of the sky. Why? I am not sure. Perhaps it was a sickness or a weakness or just a scary moment. Mother Nature can be very scary, and many of these baby creatures have a tough row to hoe, with the odds stacked against them.

I was really worried about this little fellow. I thought his tail looked a little funny. I recently saw the Disney/Pixar movie *Finding Nemo* and thought about the little baby angelfish with the bad fin.

My first inclination was to place Barney on the branch of a two-year-old tulip poplar and just walk away. But he still looked petrified, and I didn't really want to leave him there exposed so. Mary suggested I just take him back to the barn, where his home must be. Perhaps his parents would find him there, and then he would have a better chance of survival.

I cupped the little fellow in my hands once again and walked back to the barn. He didn't want to leave my hand, so I petted his head and talked with him for a while. Big recording star and author out here talking softly to a barn swallow. I felt like Snow White. I put him on a shelf of wood about five feet off the ground and said goodbye to him.

I boarded the tractor and headed back to the weedy field, where I rode around in loud circles for about six hours. This is a ten-hour field so I would not finish today. Besides I had to leave that night for a four-day trip. I thought of little Barney and hoped he was doing okay.

I saw a Mommy Doe and her little fawn walking by the woods line. I called Mary on my walkie-talkie, and she drove the truck back to see them. She also brought me some much-needed water and a BLT sandwich on toast, with fresh homegrown tomatoes. Hey, now!

Watching the fawn reminded me to be vigilant, so I cut this field so as not to run over any babies. I swear if I ever hit a fawn with this tractor I would sell the farm. My neighbor Harold told me a sweet story once about hitting a fawn and taking it to a friend who was knowledgeable enough in these matters to care for the little deer and nurse it back to health. Except for a lost ear, the deer healed up pretty well so, after about six months, he let it go back to the woods.

Well, it came to pass while my friend was deer hunting a few years later (an interesting paradox, huh?), that he had a big doe in his sights, and in that moment he noticed a missing ear. Big, tough, farm boy broke down crying, went home, and didn't hunt anymore that year.

I stopped the tractor well before entering the barn. It was about 7 p.m. I slowly approached the open barn doors and proceeded to look all over for Barney. I took it as good news that he wasn't still there sitting on the shelf. He wasn't on the barn floor anywhere either. After a while I pulled the tractor inside, shut her down, and closed up the barn.

Around the end of September the barn swallows just disappear. All of a sudden they are gone for good. I sadly take down the nests from around the house and clean up the porch. Time to get ready for the coming winter. I always miss the diving, flying spectacles that play out in my front yard every day. I kind of miss the constant chirping and early morning squawking that commences in the feathered commune around 5 a.m.

I don't know where they go. Probably Capistrano or someplace, but wherever it is, I hope that Barney is with them. I hope he has achieved his colors and has learned to fly. I hope his little forked tail is doing okay, and next March, when the cycle begins again, perhaps one of the many barn swallows buzzing around my head will be Barney.

Maybe he will know me. Maybe I'll recognize his funny tail.

Maybe I have lost my ever-loving mind!

Fly on!

A NOTHING DAY

Today I spent the whole day alone in solace and solitude. It is January third in the brand new year of our Lord, two thousand and five, and by next week at this time I will be back to singing with the Boys. Our little vacation time will be over. Just like that, my singing partners and I will be up to our eyeballs in planning meetings, music meetings, recording sessions, and getting a real good start on the new American Journey Tour, which will be coming your way before the year is over, no matter where you live!

But today is just a nothing day for me. I drove out to my farm late last night, woke up early, and started the day by playing a bit of banjo. One can play loud and long in the midst of a nothing day, especially when there is no other human being within three miles. Can you say "Clinch Mountain Backstep" with an up-the-neck break?" Yeeeeeeeeeee!

I then spent a couple of hours working on my new novel, which may either end up as a bestseller or it might stay right here on my hard drive. One never knows about these things for certain. This little book is about a lone-wolf special ops soldier by the name of Barlow and is more of a romance than a story of war. There is a good dose of magic mixed in as well.

I am a long way from completing this little epic, which was born on our recent Christmas tour in a moment of lonely imaginings. The story, when complete, could just end up as a mere steppingstone in the creative process. In other words no one may care about my characters, therefore the entire work has a chance to exist as only a good dose of practice writing. I can live with that.

After I caught up with John Barlow for a while, I went to work on some Christmas songs I am trying to write. "Christmas Morning,"

"The One," and an old one called "Uncle Luther Made the Stuffin'," which I am redoing with a bluegrass feel. Surprise, surprise!

I felt I had written some good stuff on these tunes, but nothing great had really manifested itself so far, so I aborted the laptop and the old banjer and proceeded to head on outside, where I would spend the rest of the day doing nothing.

It rained lightly off and on, but I was undeterred in my quest to clear my mind and just enjoy the quietness of my little piece of God's earth, which He has so graciously lent to me.

I walked for miles. I sat alone by the creek. I spent an hour sitting in my upper barn watching it rain. I sat by a pond for an hour, and then I walked some more. I saw seven mourning doves on three different occasions and this bothered me. There should have been eight. These timid birds are always in pairs that stay together forever, and when they flock together the number is always an even one. How did number 8 meet his end? I wondered.

How do any of us meet our end? On the other side of the world right now there are over 155,000 bodies who met their end in the fierce upheaval of a force way bigger than any of us.

What a staggering number of souls going home at one time.

Hard for us to imagine the enormity of this loss of human life unless we were there. Otherwise, it just looks kind of like something on television. I wish that it were just some obscure TV show, but the horror and loss are all too real.

May God bless all of them!

It would seem that just one missing dove caused this flood of thought and prayer on this nothing day. The mind and heart evolve and just open up sometimes. How wonderful it is to roll with that flow and allow the juices of emotion or the wine of enlightenment to fill your cup to overflowing. It can only happen to you in moments like this, when you are quiet and willing to listen. God speaks to us all the time, but we are not paying attention all the time.

I have had nothing days many times in my life, sometimes spent on a beach staring at the ocean for hours on end, sometimes anchored in a cove on the lake just watching the sunset.

As the sun goes down this evening, I have retired once again to my laptop in order to write down these few thoughts. My Mary will join me tomorrow, and we will knock down some cedar trees and clean up some flood debris from a few pastures unless it really rains. Then we will do something else.

However, today and tonight I am alone with my thoughts and my music and my musings, and I am very happy and content in my own personal skin.

Each and every moment is a precious gift from God that is not taken for granted by your writer. Each breath I take is one more adventure in this vapor of life that the book of James says is passing by, oh, so very quickly.

There is plenty of time for moving and shaking and being busy, my friends. We all have much to do in this busy world. A good thing. Hard work and personal responsibility are important and can be very gratifying. I am anxious and excited about all of the challenges and opportunities that lie ahead in this New Year, and I anticipate quite a bit of hard work!

But remember, once in a great while or as often as you can that it is so very important to get away.

To be alone.

To reflect.

To pray.

To focus.

To appreciate.

To love.

I have come to enjoy these moments more than ever because I have grown to realize that these kind of nothing days are really *something!*

THE PHIGHTING PHILLIES

October 1, 2001

Many times when the Oaks are off the road for a few days, Mary and I head out of Hendersonville to our farm, where we work and play hard, and try to clear our minds a bit. Kind of like mini-vacations.

It was a beautiful day at the farm, somewhere around seventy-six degrees and sunny. Mary spent the day watering trees, picking tomatoes, planting some shrubs, and sanding and painting two rocking chairs. I spent the whole day perched upon my John Deere 5410 tractor, pulling a ten-foot cutter around the back pastures.

We had Gypsy, one of our kitties, with us on this trip. She has not been well lately and is on several medications. Three pills twice a day. I have to rely on all of my old veterinarian assistant skills from my early teen years to accomplish this almost impossible feat. However, with the help of Mother Mary, and literally no cooperation at all from Gypsy, we seemed to enjoy about an eighty-five percent success rate, and that is relatively good.

In my *Molly The Cat* book series, I made Gypsy out to be quite the grouch, but as she has gotten older with her health failing, she has mellowed quite a bit. I refer to her now by her Gladiator name Gypsius. She doesn't seem to mind.

After a wonderful dinner, the full moon began to rise up above the cool evening and light up the countryside all around us. Our home is in a valley—or holler—and two and one half miles of Salt Lick Creek winds its way all around our pastures and woods. On most evenings a spooky fog rises off the creek and enshrouds us. The full moon reflecting off the impending fog is a real sight to see, and for a while we just sat on the porch and watched as we listened for coyotes and killdeer, who seem to make a lot of noise when the moon is full.

Sometimes we will cruise the grounds late at night in our little all-terrain John Deere Gator. We call it the midnight Gator ride, although it can happen as early as nine. The kids and grandkids especially enjoy this tradition because we always see deer and lots of stars shining on these trips.

Another tradition is the one-mile walk after dinner. It is half a mile to our front gate. We walk up to the gate, touch it, and walk back to the house. We learned this tradition from President George and Barbara Bush while visiting their home in Kennebunkport, Maine, on several occasions.

On this night Mary and Gypsy went to bed early and fell asleep while watching an auction on the Home and Garden Network, and I stretched out on the couch and tuned in Monday Night Football on the dish. The Jets were playing the Niners in the first home game in the Meadowlands of New Jersey since the terrorist attacks on the World Trade Center and the Pentagon on September 11, 2001. There was a moving ceremony during the pre-game, complete with New York City firemen and policemen carrying huge American flags, while choking back tears. Huge NFL football players were also weeping openly, as was I.

I said a prayer and thanked God for the blessings of living in the USA and asked Him to help and guide our young president, George W. Bush, in the days, weeks, and months ahead. I thought of my mother, fighting diabetes with every fiber of her being in Pennsylvania, and of my daddy, Joseph S. Bonsall, Sr., whose body rests beneath the hallowed ground of Arlington National Cemetery. He, as well as those resting all around him, paid an enormous price for the freedoms we enjoy today. Regular, hardworking guys who gathered up and fought their guts out for you and me and our families.

Now the focus in our country has returned to regular guys again. Hardworking, everyday, real men, who became our heroes once again on September 11. God bless them all!

The football game began, but it was hard to focus on touchdowns and yardage gained at this point. Besides, it wasn't the Eagles or the Tennessee Titans who were playing. I thought about going on to bed with Mary and Gypsy, but first an American male ritual. A quick surf around and through a couple hundred stations to make sure I wasn't missing anything of relevance! Mary was in bed, so I could do this freely without hearing, "Give me that. You are driving me crazy!"

Ah, the fun parts of marriage. The way I figure it, being the master of the remote control unit is a vital part of my job as a husband.

Flip. CNN, Fox News. Flip. Weather Channel, infomercial, all three networks (football on ABC of course, but I already knew that!). Flip. Snake Channel (all snakes all the time). Flip. The Food Channel (all food all the time). Flip. ESPN, baseball scores, and highlights. Cool! Six games to play and the Phillies are just two behind the Braves. Barry Bonds has sixty-nine home runs and could eclipse Mark Maguire, who eclipsed Roger Maris, who eclipsed Babe Ruth. (I just love saying the word *eclipsed!*) Then something wonderful happened. Flip. ESPN Classic.

ESPN Classic was rebroadcasting game four of the World Series from Veterans Stadium in Philadelphia, Pennsylvania, from October 20, 1993! The Phillies were playing the Toronto Blue Jays in a game that would set several World Series records. The most runs ever scored in a post-season game, and the longest nine-inning game in history. The Jays would win 15 to 14 and take a commanding three-games-to-one lead over the Phils in the '93 series. But that was not important now.

I was actually at that game on that cold and rainy night! Sitting in the left field stands just to the fair side of the foul pole, Mary and I cheered along with both my parents!

Mary, Mommy, and I sat right together—and Daddy sat directly behind us in his wheelchair in the handicapped section. Mommy booed Ricky Henderson, who was playing right below us in left field. Ricky shot an obscene gesture at the fans from behind his back, and we all rode him pretty hard throughout the whole game, especially my mother.

"Hey, this is Philly. If you can't take the heat, get your wise butt on back to the dugout!"

My mother could be a real piece of work. Once, way back in 1978, I took her to an Eagles-Giants wild-card playoff game, and she almost got me killed. Our seats were way up at the top of the Vet just five rows beneath the famous Sunoco sign, and we were surrounded by about one hundred New York Giants fans. After bantering back and forth for the entire first half, Lillie Bonsall told them all in no uncertain terms that they could just "get their kiesters back on the Jersey Turnpike and get on back to New York City where they came from!"

A few of these guys looked like button men from the Gambino crime family, and I was sure that when they stopped laughing, I was going to be gutted, and then thrown over the Sunoco sign, where I would splatter on a pretzel stand below. The last thing I would see would be a miniature Ron Jaworski throwing a long, incomplete pass to a miniature Harold Carmichael, and then boom—mustard and salt. Thankfully, old Luca Brazzi kept laughing as I made myself smaller and smaller.

But on this night there were no enemy Toronto fans for my mother to jump on, so she just aimed her wrath at Ricky Henderson. My father laughed and laughed and booed the Phillies as well as the Blue Jays. He always loved to boo the Phils just to get on my nerves.

By the time this one was over, though, everyone was booing the Phillies, including me. Reliever Mitch Williams was no Tug McGraw. He blew a huge lead and gave up five runs in the eighth inning. He was so hated in Philly after that debacle that he ended up buying a gun. He never could hit anyone though. All his shots were high and away. (*Ba Boom!*)

As the game went on longer and longer and we all began to get damper and colder, I turned around to check on Daddy and just ask if he was okay. He got defensive and teary-eyed because he thought I meant that we should leave and go home now—and he did not want to leave that ballgame. He was having such a wonderful time.

I will never forget him sitting there in his wheelchair wearing his Phillies jacket and red Phillies cap with rainwater dripping off the bill and onto his lap and into the one beer that we would let him have. I had just bought him the cap. It was very cool. It had the World Series '93 logo on the side. I still have it.

My father and I had a stormy relationship throughout most of my early years. He never seemed to understand me at all, and I must admit a lot of years and bad feelings passed by before I ever made any effort to understand where he was coming from either. In fact, it was long after his debilitating stroke, which paralyzed him and took his speech, at age thirty-nine, that I began to realize that the man was just doing the best he could all those years. And that the war had really made quite a mess out of a young nineteen-year-old from North Philly. That is no excuse for the drinking that took place from time to time. It is just a fact.

But in our worst times the Philadelphia Phillies always seemed to bridge the gap and bring us closer together. I loved the Phillies. Most years they were not very good, but I loved them. The most glorious words that I could hear as a young boy were these.

"Hey, you want to go to a game tomorrow?"

"Sure, Dad! Thanks!"

Whoa, no sleep that night. Connie Mack Stadium, hot dogs, green grass, brown infield, those wonderful red and white uniforms, the smell of cigars, the crack of the bat, the pop of the glove.

"Hey, there's Richie Ashburn, son, and there's Johnny Callison. Wow, there's the Pittsburgh Pirates. Boooooooo!" Heaven was just seventy blocks away at Twenty-first and Lehigh.

He usually took me to a game on a Sunday. If Dad were to have gotten called into work on Saturday night, the plan could be in trouble. He was a maintenance man and chief electrician, and if the plant called with a breakdown, he just might go to a bar after work and down enough Boilermakers that he would be tempted to stay away until Monday—or maybe Tuesday.

Mom always called these wondrous events binges. And a binge was always a real possibility. When that happened, though, he always felt so badly about it that we would get along just wonderfully for a long time thereafter. However, I preferred a hungover father and old Shibe Park as compared to, "Sorry, kiddo, I'll make it up to ya next time."

Mommy always made us go to church with her, meaning my sister Nancy and me—not Joseph Sr., although Daddy went to church on a few Easters over the years. I would be singing a solo in church, so Mommy would kind of shame him into going. On a rare Sunday he would make lunch for us. It was really breakfast, but he would have it on the table when we arrived home from church.

The word *brunch* never occurred to us on Jasper Street. He would prepare either pancakes (much better than Mom's) or shit-on-ashingle, a white gravy and dried beef concoction poured over toast. It was an army thing and I loved it.

"You wouldn't love it if you *had* to eat it," he would laugh.

On a day like that, after fidgeting around all morning at Sunday school and morning service at the Calvary Church of the Brethren, eating Dad's SOS and heading for the game were some of the great moments of my life. How amazing it is that the man who at times could make me feel so absolutely awful could also make me feel like the luckiest kid on earth by uttering these ten magic words: "Get in the car, son. Curt Simmons is pitching today!"

This is where my writing stops. I am not sure where I am going with the entire project or even what direction it will take in the future, but for now this part works and even seems relevant at the moment. You see, Connie Mack Stadium, or Shibe Park as locals called it, is long gone, and now the Vet will be turned into a parking lot as well. Daddy and Mommy are also gone, but the Phighting Phillies play on.

Next year they will begin to play in a brand new ball yard. Johnny Callison, Richie Ashburn, Robin Roberts as well as Tug McGraw, Pete Rose, and Mike Schmidt are all just memories. New guys with name like Rollins, Byrd, Burrell, and Thome are the new Phillies who will begin to build new memories in a new park.

I can see a young nine-year-old boy with a Phillies hat sitting almost sideways on his head. His ball glove hangs off his left hand and he holds a hot dog in his right. He is sitting next to his father at the new Citizens Bank Ballpark. The green grass and the white lines are mesmerizing, and look at that! There they are—the Phillies! Red pinstripes on a snow-white uniform. And look, Dad—the Pittsburgh Pirates! *Booooooo*!

Nothing really changes. Thank God!

Addendum

In 2008 the Philadelphia Phillies won their second World Series ever by beating the upstart Tampa Rays in a rain-soaked affair that ended in victory for all us Philly kids who have lived our entire lives following this storied team. As I write this, it is October 2009, and miracle of miracles, the Phillies are going to the World Series again. This time they will do battle with the New York Yankees. Could it happen again? World Champions? Rollins, Victorino, Utley, Howard, Werth, Ibanez, Hamels, Lidge, et al.

The last time the Phils played the Yanks in the World Classic was in 1950, when Robin Roberts' tired arm gave way to a Yankee sweep over the Philly Whiz Kids. I was just two years old, but I think I can still hear my father booing the team!

Are you watching, Mommy and Daddy? Are you watching? Go Phillies!!

This story was written about a year before my father passed away and long before G.I. Joe and Lilllie *was written. I dedicate this little story to Joe Sr., my mom, Lillie, and my precious sister, Nancy.*

A TRIP BACK HOME

I drove back into the old neighborhood today. The Oak Ridge Boys had a day off in Hershey, Pennsylvania, so I rented a Toyota Corolla at the Harrisburg airport and drove across the Pennsylvania countryside to the little town of Spring City. This is the home of the Southeastern Pennsylvania Veterans Center, where my Mom and Dad, both veterans of WWII, now reside.

It was a very bright and sunny spring afternoon, and I was so happy that my concert schedule worked out in such a way that I would be allowed see my folks. Usually a day off is spent in some town a long ways off, with nothing to do but take a walk and watch the corn grow. Today worked out just right.

I parked the rental car in the main lot and proceeded to the fourth floor of the veterans home. Mom was upbeat as usual, and Dad was downbeat as usual, although I cannot blame him. His old stroke-ridden body is so frail now, and besides that he just had a toe removed and he is in pain from a bout with the shingles. Otherwise, I guess he is doing just great!

I took Mom out to dinner and Wal-Mart, which was a big day for her. I bought Daddy a singing fish called Billy Bass or something goofy like that. Anyhow, it sang "Don't Worry, Be Happy" and he laughed so hard that he almost fell out of bed. Well worth the $22.50 for the singing fish.

I said goodbye to them both and headed on into the City of Brotherly Love. Late Sunday afternoon, as I exit the Schulkyll

Expressway and turn onto U.S. Route 1 North, I notice that the sun is just now beginning to sink behind William Penn's hat on top of city hall in center city Philadelphia. I have to chuckle at this point. The statue of Penn on top of city hall collects rainwater in a storm, and it drains off the hat in such a way that if you stand on South Broad Street and look up, Mr. Penn appears to be taking a hearty, colonial piss on downtown Philly. I swear it is true. Check it out sometime.

I needed that light moment. The veterans home is a wonderful facility, and my folks are truly very well taken care of there. Their years of service to this country and all the medals hanging over Daddy's bed have earned them the right to that care, and for that I am very appreciative. However, seeing them there somehow rips my heart into little pieces, and it takes days to push it all back a bit farther into my mind.

Their last several years of living in the old house was really very scary, and I worried about them constantly. Even though I had them install a complete state-of-the-art (I hate that expression) security system, and even though my sister, Nancy, lived relatively close in nearby Cherry Hill, New Jersey, the streets were getting worse and the whole neighborhood was going downhill faster every day.

Also, Mom's diabetes was getting worse. Her eyesight was failing and after a diabetic coma hit her and we almost lost her, it was time to talk serious turkey. Mom agreed and actually led the way, (as usual, in making plans for what she called the soldiers home. They have lived in the soldiers home for two years now.

One year ago today, Nancy sold the little row house that my parents had lived in for fifty years. It was paid off too, as Mom liked to say. Little Joey Bonsall grew up there, and now fifty-plus years later I find myself driving to Jasper Street for the first time in almost two years, and I am not even sure why I am doing it.

Anyhow, I exit the Roosevelt Expressway and take a left on Wingahocking Avenue. I have always chuckled at that too. Such a funny name, Wingahocking Avenue Exit, a quarter mile. Hahaha! I am so glad I never lived on that street.

On to Hunting Park Avenue. That sounds much better. Oh, you live by Hunting Park? Oh my. Well, well! How very nice.

Yeah, right!

I pass through the new complex of row houses right off of Hunting Park, where most of the residents speak Spanish and the music is pounding out of the passing cars so loudly that the street is actually shaking. When I was sixteen and jacked up the volume on my cheesy-sounding radio that dwelled inside my old winged-monster, '59 Impala, people would yell from their front porches to "turn that thing down—or off!" I would too, and I was probably only blasting, "Soldier Boy" by the Sherelles.

Nowadays kids have bad ass rap music thumping out of bass speakers, with lyrics about rape and killing. And people are just too afraid to say anything. Ah, the whiff of passing and changing times. It is not a pleasant aroma.

Anyhow, I make it through without getting shot or taken hostage. I am still quite a few blocks from my old house. I drive through Juniata. Actually it is just another several blocks of row homes, but the homes on these streets always seemed a little nicer, more well-kept. Little bitty lawns with a few azalea bushes and awnings on the windows.

When I was little I used to think that moving about fifteen blocks over to Juniata would really be moving on up. I remember when the Williamson family over on Clearance Street moved over there, taking two relatively good-looking daughters with them. Janet and Diane Williamson were moving to Juniata. To me they might as well have been moving to a new row house on the moon.

What everyone really dreamed about was moving to a home on the Jersey shore.

When I was a kid that was the ultimate goal of the hard-working people in the old neighborhood. To live down at da shore! Atlantic City, Wildwood, Ocean City, Cape May—hey, it really didn't matter. Just to live at da shore. I don't believe that I ever saw the Williamson girls again after their big move to Juniata. I can also honestly say that I never remember anyone actually moving to da shore either.

Past Juniata, down K Street to Kensington Avenue. Ah, getting close now. Cross Kensington and go under the EL. The Elevated Frankford Commuter Train was called the EL when it ran aboveground and the subway when it ran beneath the ground. That seemed to always make sense, and one thing that did not change was the sound of the EL pulling into the Tioga Street station just one block from where I grew up.

I pulled over and listened. The sound of those iron wheels on the tracks as they slowed to a halt was indeed a sound of childhood, and, hey, they have even remodeled the old EL station. When I was a kid, the old Tioga Street EL station was where bums hung out. They are called homeless, now I guess, but back then we called them bums. They are the reason that the old EL station smelled like stale pee. On a hot, muggy summer day, yo, it was rough. I'll bet the new station still smells a little like pee. It just has to. You could get on that train and go right on in to downtown Philly or go the other way and end up in Frankford, where I went to high school. Either way, you held your nose while digging for a token.

On a musical note, the EL station had great acoustics. Guys would gather down there and sing harmony. We all sounded good as our voices echoed off the walls, and the bums seemed to really enjoy it.

By now you have noticed that each inner-city neighborhood has its own name, and in reality each has its own personality and identity too. This city is really made up of small towns that are entities all to themselves, with names like Fishtown, Kensington, Frankford, Harrowgate, and on and on. As a teenager I was involved in some pretty big fights defending the local turf. Basically the young guys all fought for Kensington because Harrowgate was a part of Kensington.

The main intersection was Kensington and Allegheny avenues, which was three blocks from the Tioga EL station. There was an Allegheny Avenue EL station, too, that also smelled like pee. Many of us were part of the K & A gang, which is another story for sure. For now I'll just tell you that we really were a pretty tough bunch, especially when we hung out with the older, really bad-ass K & A guys.

We would gather on the corner of Atlantic and Jasper streets, jump in some old cars that belonged to the older guys, and drive over to Juniata or Fishtown to fight for good old K & A. And I usually got my clock cleaned.

I used to think it was so funny that guys would get so bent out of shape over a few concrete streets. We were much like alley cats staking out our territory. I always figured, however, that if war were to ever break out between Philly and, say, Trenton, New Jersey, or Baltimore (or maybe even Camden), all these guys would gather together as one big army and march down Interstate 95 in Phillies hats and Eagles helmets shouting yo and eating cheesesteaks and soft pretzels.

I grew up on Jasper Street, which was right by Harrowgate Square. The little park was looked over by the city department of recreation, and I mean, just that. The city would mow around the WWII Memorial on the Kensington Avenue side from time to time, but for the most part, it was just looked over.

Neighborhood folks called it da square. It was, in reality, one square block of grass, trees, and dog poop. But to little boys it became a ballpark or a football stadium or even a boxing ring with just a slight turn of the imagination.

By the way, each neighborhood had a string band and the Harrowgate String Band was one of the best in the city. On rare occasions they would put on a concert in da square, and everybody would come out to hear them. These bands were a very strange phenomenon and remain a part of Philly folklore to this day. They were made up of average neighborhood guys who would dress up in huge, feathered outfits and play old songs like "Oh Dem Golden Slippers" on banjos while drinking whiskey from a hip flask.

Each New Year's Day string bands from all over the Delaware Valley would gather to march and dance through downtown Philly in front of thousands of people and a nationwide TV audience. It is still a huge event that is called the Mummers Parade, which is kind of like a weird Mardi Gras for guys who hang out in bars.

This city is so fascinating to me. Guys who would knock your block off at an Eagles game dress up in purple feathers and funny shoes and enthusiastically play the living daylights out of banjos and xylophones while doing a silly dance called the Mummers Strut. There is even a Mummers Hall of Fame. All of this, mind you, from the same city that gave us *American Bandstand*.

So I drive on under the EL across Kensington Avenue and proceed one block down Venango Street to Jasper and turn right. I slowly drive past three small blocks of row houses, garages, alleyways, and trash, and pull over to the curb and park directly across the street from the old house. I roll down the driver's side window and just sit there.

To my right is a vacant corner lot piled with trash that was once Del's Restaurant, where actual mob guys came to eat. It was amazing!

At lunchtime there would be Cadillacs and Lincolns parked on the street where normally there were just the Fords and Chevys that belonged to the blue-collar working men who lived in these homes. Now old Del's was just a pile of rat-infested rubbish.

A few years ago I had taken part in the Presidents' Summit on Volunteerism program that was held right here in Philly. The Oaks and former President George Bush actually went into a section of Germantown and cleaned up a few streets with the help of a bunch of nice inner-city kids. Presidents, generals, and volunteers spread out all across Philadelphia to clean up the streets in order to inspire people to keep them clean, to volunteer, and to mentor young people. It was a great event, and I believe that a lot of good took place. However, they missed this section of Harrowgate, one block from Kensington and the EL, and they sure as hell missed old Del's corner.

I sit in my rented Corolla and stare over at the two-story home at 3517 Jasper Street. I would like to say that the sinking sun was shining on the second floor and that there were happy faces of young children playing on the porch while Mom cooked Salisbury steak and Dad showered the factory grease off while smoking a Winston. (I have to say that my father actually smoked while taking a bath.)

But no, none of these things were true. The house was shut up and dark and still looked pretty much the same as the day when Nancy and I loaded "GI Joe and Lillie" into an ambulance for their last ride down Jasper Street on their way to Spring City and the soldiers home.

In my mind's eye I could see Joey sitting on the porch with Mommy and dear old Nana Clark. I could see my sister posing in her brand new Easter dress. I could see Daddy's latest brand-new used car parked by the telephone pole.

I could see a young teenage Joey sitting on the corner of what was then Flannery's candy store with about eight other guys who were just as energetic and confused as he was. I see a boy running down the street all bloodied up from a fistfight that he lost and trying hard not to cry.

I see a young Lillie standing on the corner yelling over towards Harrowgate Park "Joeeeyyyyy" at the top of her lungs, hoping for a response from the dirty little kid wearing a Phillies' hat and playing ball. I see my father park his Studebaker, and then—thanks to a good mix of

Seagrams Seven and Ballantine Beer—not be able to get out of it and walk to the house, so he stays in the car and sleeps while his dinner gets cold.

As long as I sit here, these images and mirages constantly appear and fade. I feel as if Rod Serling is looking over my shoulder. I also feel as if I am stuck here in somewhat of a time warp, an hourglass slowly running out of sand.

Strangely enough, my whole thought pattern is interrupted by some goofy girl in a white miniskirt with purple lips, multi-colored hair, and a nose ring. She is pounding on the passenger side window and saying something. I roll the window down so as to hear this pearl of wisdom.

"Hey, are ya dating?" she asks.

I almost break out laughing.

"Yer not a cop are ya?"

That is even funnier—a fifty-two-year-old cop in an Avis rental Corolla. Now that would really have been undercover.

Then I notice the five guys not far behind her and my Spidey sense kicks in a bit. (It always worked for Peter Parker.) I am bit scared; however, I kind of feel like jumping out of this stupid looking little gray car and kicking some honest-to-God, old-time Philly ass!

This old neighborhood was far from perfect when I was growing up here. The families that occupied these little homes had their share of trouble, and ours was no exception. Some worked in various factories. Some were truck drivers, policemen, firemen, and such. They were all tough blue-collar guys who drank and smoked too much. Most of them fought in the wars from Normandy to Iwo Jima to Korea, and they still maintained at least some sort of pride in themselves.

June Cleaver didn't live here either. However, I remember so many wonderful mothers like my own who worked two jobs to help make ends meet and raised families and did the best they could. I grew up here and learned a lot of harsh lessons and, quite honestly, I was learning more today.

That old phrase "everything changes, everything stays the same" does not apply to the corner of Jasper and Tioga. Nothing here is the same. Flannery's Candy Store, Elmer's Hardware, Russock's Drug Store, Mrs. Tuma's Dry Cleaning and Emrich's Grocery Store are long gone. Progress Manufacturing, Craftex Textiles, Schlicters Steel

Mill and many others have long since vanished. The Midway and Iris Theaters have been replaced by a McDonalds and a Blockbuster video store.

Now, don't get me wrong. I know in my heart that there are still a lot of good, honest, hardworking people around who, like the generations before them, are also doing the best they can. It is just that I wonder if the dreams are still there. I hope so.

I once walked these streets with a head and heart chock full of dreams and plans and goals that I would someday accomplish. Where are the dreams of this young hooker and these hard-bodied thugs behind her, smoking pot and listening to Snoop Doggy?

The trash in the streets speaks volumes about lost pride, and it makes me so sad on one level. However, a voice screams out inside my heart that is thanking my Almighty God for the veterans home and thanking Him for His constant, guiding hand on my life all these years.

A wave of common sense prevails and I do not jump out of the car.

"Gotta go," I tell the young street girl as the neighborhood darkens. "Why don't you guys clean up around here a little?" I yell as I lay Toyota rubber on Jasper Street.

Whoa, big tough Philly Boy. I am laughing again. I used to think that I could move back to the city anytime, and I guess I could if I had to; however, it would take a Supreme Court decision to ever pry me away from the rolling hills of Tennessee.

I drive over the Betsy Ross Bridge and have dinner with my wonderful sister in Jersey. We were always such a small ship— Mommy, Daddy, Nancy, and Joey. And I love my sister so very much. In fact, I love her more than ever.

"Went by the old house on the way here."

"Neighborhood is awful, isn't it?" she replies.

"Why did Mommy stay there so long? God knows I tried to get her to move out for years," I said.

"Old school, Joey, you know that. She worked hard, annnndddd—"

"It was paid off!" We said it in perfect unison, while laughing out loud.

Nancy made me a wonderful dinner. We laughed and cried and said goodbye. I drove in the darkness for three hours and sang songs. Old rock-and-roll songs, some Springsteen, and a few gospel tunes. I sang so hard I really didn't have much voice left for the show the next night.

By 2 a.m. I was back in a Hershey, Pennsylvania, hotel room, tucked hard into bed and dreaming about hitting a baseball over the park benches in our make-believe Connie Mack Stadium at Harrowgate Square. The black electrical tape around the old ball makes it hard to find as dusk settles and the tree branches start to meld in with the sky. I circle the bases, laughing. A tree is first base, second base is a mound of dirt, third is a light pole, and home plate is a strategically placed paper bag.

I stomp hard on the bag and my mother's voice fills the air. "Joeeeeyyyy, come on home and eat! Your father and Nancy are already at the table." She sounds a little like Lucille Ball in my dream.

"Coming Maaaaaaa!" I yell as I pick up my old Adirondack bat and my Jimmy Piersall-model Wilson glove and head across Tioga Street toward home.

Old Del is sweeping leaves off of his sidewalk, and he waves at me as I cross the street and disappear inside the little two-story row house at 3517 Jasper Street.

THE LEGEND OF THE LOST IPHONE

The Oak Ridge Boys went to Philly to premiere our new *The Boys Are Back* CD on QVC. It turned out to be a tremendous idea. We pre-sold over 7,000 copies.

But for me it was visiting the hometown of my youth. I had a ball. After the QVC show, my precious sister Nancy and I, along with her husband Chuck, went to a late dinner at a five-star Italian restaurant. Around midnight, we loaded Sherman Halsey (Jim's son), our tour director Darrick Kinslow, and William Lee Golden into a car and drove around the old neighborhood streets where Joey and Nancy grew up with "G. I. Joe and Lillie."

The last time I wrote a commentary about Philly ("A Trip Back Home"), I wrote in detail about how dirty everything was. Now don't get me wrong, my old neighborhood has turned out to be not so desirable, and I would almost be afraid to step back into the house at 3517 Jasper Street. But the streets were much cleaner on this visit. The trash bags and broken bottles and junk were gone as a result of Philly Mayor Nutter's clean up the city campaign. Nice job, Mr. Mayor. I hope it lasts. (I know it will not!)

WLG took a ton of pictures, as did D. K. and I. We saw some strange sights while driving around the Harrowgate and Kensington areas late at night.

An old corner tavern had turned Hispanic. It probably used to be called the Shamrock or something similar, but now it is painted yellow with the words *El Bar* painted on the side of the building. There were about six guys inside, all bellied up to the bar.

One could easily get killed in there, I am certain. Funny picture, though. There is nothing in my DNA that would encourage me to paint a building yellow!

93

Another funny sight (kind of) was a homeless man pushing a grocery cart down the street with a Jacuzzi in it! You just do not see that every day. Sherman was on the floor, even though he is from LA and has seen almost everything. (He was still raised in Kansas, Toto.) For him and old Alabama boy Golden and Kentucky Boy Darrick, this ride was a huge awakening. Much like Lillie in the book when Joe first took her to the home of his childhood, these guys were probably thinking, *He grew up here?*

Yes, I did!

The little Joey who roamed these streets, played baseball in these parks, and blasted his stereo in his little row house bedroom grew up here! I am not trying to plug a book here, but if you read *G.I. Joe and Lillie*, there is quite a bit in there about growing up at 3517 Jasper Street in the 50s and early 60s.

The next day—a miracle! Nancy picked up Darrick and me, and we again drove all over the city. I showed DK where I went to school, played ball, got into fights, and where I worked. We then toured the sports complexes and South Philly, where we stopped at Tony Luke's and ate pizza steaks. Darrick had never eaten such a thing in his life and will probably never eat one again. I ate two!

We also loaded up on some soft pretzels—the Philly kind!—right out of the oven from the pretzel factory on Oregon Street. Yum! Then we drove downtown, where my sister guarded the car while DK and I jumped out to see the Joe Bonsall *Philadelphia Music Hall of Fame* plaque that is implanted in the sidewalk on Broad Street across from the Academy of Music. I knelt down and Darrick took pictures. What I did not realize was that right there around my name in stone I dropped my iPhone. We jumped in the car and went back to the hotel, and I almost threw up when I reached for it and it was not there. I hate to admit to addiction, but . . . ummm . . .

My sister was on her way back over the Ben Franklin Bridge to Jersey when D. K. called her to see if it might be in the car. It was not! I sat in my hotel room trying not to be depressed and calling my own number. After a while, a man with an accent answered the iPhone. I told him the phone was mine and asked if he would consider returning it to me. I told him I would take a cab anywhere to meet him, and he said, "No, I will bring it to your hotel. I am in West Philly and on a yellow bike."

I have an "if lost please call" app on the phone and found out later that he called my wife Mary just before I called him.

A while later, a tall black man with a Jamaican accent pulled up to the hotel on a yellow bike, his Rasta hairdo tucked under a helmet and a huge friendly smile on his face. He handed me the iPhone. He told me his name was Chester.

I said, "You rode a bike from West Philly to here? We are as far east as one can get in this city without falling into the Delaware!"

Chester said, "That is what I do, sir. I ride!"

Indeed he does.

He climbed back on his bike, and I told him how much this meant to me on many levels. I told him I would never forget him and gave him $200.

His first impulse was to hand it back to me, and then he started to cry. Big tears rolled right down, out of both eyes, like Demi Moore in the movie *Ghost*.

"You just do not know how much I can use this," he said in a choked accent. He said thank you and boarded his yellow bike and rode off.

I consider it a small miracle that a fancy iPhone dropped in the middle of downtown Philly during rush hour was back in my hands within an hour, but I must also tell you that I believe that most people would have returned the phone if they could, because most people are decent. Most people will do the right thing almost every time. I know I would, and I know the guys I travel with every day would as well. I remember finding a wallet once on a street in Phoenix. It was full of credit cards and about $240. Well, I got it back to the guy!

God blesses you, and it always comes back. I hope he blesses Chester the same way.

All in all that was a pretty nice trip back to the City of Brotherly Love. Hey, it's a tough town and that moniker does not always fit. But that day it did.

A FINE LINE

I just heard a very well-known television preacher go on and on and *on* about the sins and retributions of the Harry Potter book series and movies. I listened with interest as he admonished anyone who would read these books and instructed every parent in his church and in the realm of his voice to ban Potter from their children's thoughts and forbid them to go to the movies or to watch them on TV. The Harry Potter books were denounced as Satanism, pure and simple, and would, therefore, cause kids and adults alike to turn away from the Bible, Christ, and the church. One would think that author J. K. Rowling just might be the Antichrist!

As a Bible-believing Christian, I tried hard to sort all this out in my heart and mind. I am one of the few who have not read even one Harry Potter book, but I have seen most of the movies and must admit I enjoyed them very much. I marvel at the fact that the young actor who plays Potter almost seems to be approaching thirty years old, yet he and his cohorts have still not graduated from that school. A degree in wizardry must be really tough to obtain.

In my heart I do not believe that Harry and the fantasies created by Ms. Rowling will send us packing for hell. If you notice, just like in all the old fairytales, westerns, and even most horror tales, the good always wins over the bad.

I am thrilled that children are actually reading a book or two instead of being planted in front of a video game system or Facebook for hours upon hours.

But I want to give this fine preacher his due. Much of the media that our children are exposed to in this day and age does or has the potential to provide a negative effect on their upbringing. I think Viagra commercials during the evening news at dinnertime are a bit more unsettling than Harry and his fellow wizard students.

But enough of Mr. Potter. The question still remains: Just how much do sex and violence in movies, TV, and video games really affect the young minds and hearts that are watching them?

I am not claiming to have a viable answer to this age-old question, but for just a moment I would like to share a relevant piece of backstory with you.

When I was a boy growing up in Philadelphia, both my parents worked to make ends meet. You may have read about Nana Clark in my book *G.I. Joe and Lillie*. Well, Gertrude Clark was a feisty old woman who rented our upstairs back bedroom and became my mentor and best friend as I was growing up. She, along with my precious mother, Lillie, was a constant and positive force in my life.

One of the great things Nana did was to encourage me to read! Between the ages of seven and twelve, I devoured so many books and stories that my imagination ran wild every single day. From *Grimm's Fairy Tales* (of which many were much scarier then the evil Valdemort, as I recall) to Zane Gray westerns, to all of H. G. Wells, Jules Verne, and Jack London novels.

I remember reading the original Bram Stoker *Dracula* book and not being able to sleep for about a week. Count Dracula in the book was much scarier then the cartoonish vampire portrayed on film by Bela Lugosi. Mary Shelly's *Frankenstein* also scared the pants off me, but it certainly did not do any damage. I never once started to bite people on the neck or want to start digging up graves.

These stories took me to the old West, to Alaska, to the Moors of London, and even to Transylvania. They instilled in me a desire to learn more about the world that existed outside the streets of my neighborhood. As music became more and more a part of my young life, and as I got older, the feeling of wanting to go way on out there and do something was the focal point of my being. I was not content with the status quo of the streets. I wanted more.

Now this is not an autobiography, but just a mere commentary. I will write more about the trials and tribulations of little Joey some other time, but the point is that I came out just fine. Good upbringing and a growing faith in Jesus Christ have helped me to overcome every obstacle that ever shed a negative light on my pathway.

Did I just mention good upbringing. Yes, I did. The real key to doing what is right and to not be affected by the negative is to have parents and people around you who care and take the time to teach you what is right—and what is wrong. Good parenting, or the lack thereof, is the single most influential thing affecting our children today.

I walked that fine line one day years ago when my daughter Jennifer was listening intently to a Sony Walkman cassette player (remember those?). I was not sure about the particular band she was into, so I asked if I could listen. She reluctantly surrendered to me the said Walkman, and after listening to the whole thing, I ejected the cassette and threw it into the lake.

I will not go into the lyrical content, but as a father I did not want my thirteen year old listening to those songs. It was my call as a father, and she respected that. Well, after a few years she did.

Parents' call!! Walk the fine line! You may not always make the right decision, but it is the love and caring that really matter. Children really want to know that someone loves them and has the courage to disagree with them from time to time. In reality, it is their safety net!

So in my opinion the real bottom line here is that we must do the best we can, and we must pay attention to our children. We must love them as Christ loves us.

It is a mean world out there, but it always has been. It is a more permissive society, for certain, and I believe more than ever that as parents and children alike we need Christ in our lives. Then perhaps our decisions will be shaped more by what is inside us and for us as opposed to that which is against us.

So Harry Potter? Again, it is the parents who must make the call. It is my opinion that just as in most fairy tales and westerns, where good prevails over evil, there is no harm done in reading these books. You do not have to agree with me, and that famous TV preacher certainly would not!

The relevant point is that reading and imagination, caring discussion, and love and understanding as well as positive thinking are what really matter!

I realize that not every child is as fortunate as little Joey was to have such a positive force in their life as Nana Gertrude Clark. I went to see her on her deathbed as cancer was about to win the battle. I was fourteen, and Nana was very small and wasted away. She told me she loved me, and then she passed on to Glory.

I had an asthma attack within days after her funeral that put me in the hospital. I dreamed that she was there in the room standing at the foot of my bed in the same blue dress she was buried in. She smiled at me and told me she was in heaven now and not to worry about her. She told me she would throw me a star.

To this day I am not at all certain that was just a dream, for I have never forgotten the moment. I have always believed in my heart that Nana Clark actually paid a visit to my hospital room that night on her way to Jesus. As a side note, that was the last asthma attack I ever had.

I believe in my heart that she has thrown me many a star over these years. The first one being when she first entered through the door at 3517 Jasper Street and put a book in my hand.

Yes, we walk a fine line as parents and grandparents, but urging our kids to read is a good thing.

So then, romance, war, philosophy, predictions, visions, biographies, great lessons, good versus evil, and great short stories of hope and truth and faith? Yes indeed! The Bible is a great start!

BEING JOSEPH

"We have as our special guest this morning, Joseph S. Bonsall, the author of the book *G.I. Joe and Lillie*. Good morning, Joseph, and welcome to the program. Do you prefer I call you Joseph or Joe?"

"Good morning. I am honored to be here on the air with you today. Thanks for having me. *Joe* works just fine."

"Well then . . . Joseph . . . tell us about this wonderful book."

The world of being an author promoting a book is very similar to a music act promoting a new CD. Yet I must admit, it is a little quirkier.

Over the course of my long career with the Oak Ridge Boys, I have probably spoken to several thousand country music and rock-and-roll deejays, and I still do today. But in the book promo universe I find myself speaking to a more diverse group of radio personalities, and it can sometimes be a funny trip.

Allow me to backtrack just a bit to *The Molly the Cat* book days, when I first started to collide with the literary world. All of a sudden I found myself at book fairs, booksellers' conventions, and author events. It was a whole new world for me—and a very exciting one at that.

But thankfully my tongue has always been planted deeply within the confines of my cheek because these author types really take themselves seriously. And some of the people who interview authors think and talk like the puffed-up guy on the *Inside The Actors' Studio* interview show.

There are many music people who think they are a bit above you because they sing songs for a living, but many actors, and especially authors, win the prize in the inflated-ego department. Quite frankly, I find it all to be a tremendous source of personal entertainment.

Instead of doing a lot of book signings, my publisher and I decided to plow through every day with a handful of radio interviews to promote *G.I. Joe and Lillie.* I was on the road a lot that year and every morning, either from a cell phone, on the bus, or in a motel room somewhere across the U.S. of A., you would find me talking to a diverse group of radio personalities—sometimes as many as six in one day.

Between Oaks' publicist Sanford Brokaw; the Jakasa group out of New Orleans, which was hired by New Leaf Press to set up TV and radio stuff as well as the in-house publicity departments at New Leaf and ORB, Inc., I was one busy boy. Because the Oaks were also pushing our new *Colors* CD, you can add Spring Hill Music to the group of people setting up interviews.

On a side note: The book provided a tremendous opportunity to promote *Colors* on radio shows that might not usually speak to the Oaks—such as talk radio. And the various PR firms worked together marvelously in coordinating interviews and making sure each station I talked to was well supplied with books, info, and the *Colors* CD.

There were, in fact, a lot of great TV appearances for the group and for myself, including *Hannity and Colmes, Fox News with Brit Hume,* the *Cal Thomas Show,* and The *700 Club.* We also had a fair share of newspaper coverage, including a *USA Today Weekend* story. However, it was the world of radio where I spent most of my time, and, as I said, it was a real trip.

Talk radio, country radio, religious radio, Christian talk, Southern gospel, contemporary Christian, Public Broadcasting, family talk, syndicated, taped, live, in-studio . . . on and on. Being Joseph meant being on the radio somewhere across the fruited plain several times each day, talking about *G.I. Joe and Lillie* and *Colors.*

I must say, the real blessing came when the interviewer had actually read my little book. The light came on. They understood where I was coming from with my story about the lives of my parents.

When a host had just skimmed the book or not read it at all, I ended up doing all the talking. That's fine, but it is even finer when that local radio personality is the one who goes on and on about why someone should buy the book. Ah, but again . . . the *diversity.*

Country jocks. It's usually early morning, two at a time, guy and girl. Both have been drinking coffee since 4 a.m. and are ever more hosting the morning show, wide awake and wired, while your author may have just started scooping Starbucks into the Sunbeam.

"Good morning, Dayton . . . Joe Bonsall of the Oak Ridge Boys is on the air with us, live from his farm in Tennessee, and he has a great new book called *G.I Joe and Lillie!* The Oaks also have a new patriotic-flavored CD called *Colors!* Hey, Joe, welcome to the Coyote and Susie show!"

"Uh, good morning."

"Susie, here. Hi'ya there, Joe. How are the Boys? How's Duane Allen? I interviewed him once in 1986. When are you coming to Dayton?"

"Uh, good morning."

"Great book, man!" yells Coyote. "I read it last night. Heavy, heavy-duty stuff, my friend. I never knew you could write like that."

"Yeah, what's that all about?" chimes in Susie. (Lots of laughter.)

"We have to go to a break right now, but Joe Bonsall is with us this morning, so stay tuned!"

"Uh . . . good morning."

I am of course making light of myself here. Rest assured, if I am getting up at 6 a.m. to be on Spunk radio, I *am* going to plug my book and our new CD!

I can talk even faster than they can when I get going. I have always been the master of getting my point across within whatever time frame they may provide. No matter what they ask, I always find a way.

Next call, a public radio talk show out of a major city with some introspective name like Reflections, Inside the Author's Head, or something else just as goofy.

"The book . . . *G.I. Joe and Lillie.* The author . . . Joseph S. Bonsall. Welcome, Joseph, to this premier segment of The Author Gags."

"Thank you, sir, I am honored to be here today. I can gag with the best of them."

"If you would be so kind as to share with our very sophisticated listening audience the reason, or perhaps the impetus behind, or perhaps even the metaphysical, yet guiding, force that tapped into your creative reserve and allowed you to come up with, shall we say, the proper words that describe the—I hate to be repetitive—impetus . . . as to why this book. . . . as opposed to any other book . . . "

I was starting to really miss Coyote and Susie.

One time years ago one of these pompous types asked me about "the impetus and true meaning behind the character of Gypsy in the Molly book series."

I started laughing. I couldn't help it. I was very tired at the time, and all I could picture in my mind was my big black-and-white cat, Gypsy, sitting at the foot of our bed licking her private parts. *There* was some impetus for you! I laughed so hard I cried. Mr. Pompous never did understand that interview.

Christian talk radio is usually very cool. I have been on the air with some wonderful hosts who really loved my book and gave me tons of quality time to talk about it. New Leaf Press and Spring Hill Music are both Christian companies, and they get a lot of respect from religious broadcasters. I can remember only one guy who was a real hoot.

Let's call him Doctor Stuffshirt.

"Goooood morning, Joseph . . . welcome to the show that puts Caaa-riiist first in all that we do. I assume that you know the Caaa-riiist!

"Well, yes, Doctor Shirt, I am happy to say that—"

"Because it is Caaa-riiist who comes first on this broadcast."

"As well He should, sir. My new book, *G.I. Joe and Lillie,* published by New—"

"Tell me, Joseph, is He—the Caaa-riiist—the focal point of this book?"

"Well, sir, it is a book about faith. But it is also a book about war and romance—"

"Heaven and earth . . . soon shall pass, but only what's done for Caaa-riiist will truly . . . last."

"I agree, the book chronicles the life of my parents, actually from the time they ran away from home and joined the army, up until the time they are buried in Arlingt—"

"Let us pray!"

It was the longest hour of my entire life.

I will end this little journey with my favorite story of being Joseph, which happened during the *Molly* era. *Molly, The Home,* and *Outside* were published, and the fourth book, *Brewster,* was just about to be released. I was invited to the prestigious annual Washington Press Club book event, sponsored by Barnes and Noble. About twenty-five authors of all kinds were to take part in this event.

We all sat in little cubicles, and the public came in to buy books and have them signed. All of the profits went to a D.C. children's hospital. I had spent the afternoon at the hospital handing out *Molly* books, which was very rewarding.

Before this diverse group of authors scattered to their booths to meet the public that night, there was a one-hour reception that was even covered by C-SPAN. A Perrier and cheese party, where the authors—and even some members of the press—chatted about their newest book, while daintily eating a piece of Roquefort on a cracker and sipping sparkling water. It was hilarious.

A well-dressed woman who had just written a new self help/diet/ motivational book was admiring my red-flowered tie. I told her it was a Rush Limbaugh Collection tie. She backed away from me as if I had stabbed her in the heart. She walked with a cane, and her cane started shaking. She nearly toppled into the Perrier vat.

Did I mention that the Washington Press Club leaned so far to the left that it resembled the Tower of Pisa? It was a wonder the Limbaugh tie didn't get me thrown out.

But the cake was really taken when a huge black man approached me and introduced himself as a fellow author. His rhetoric was astounding, and as he spoke his jaws actually seemed to bag out and hang down further and further.

"I have just written a new book on diiipppllloooommmacccy . . . as it relates to the blllaaaaackkk. You see, in the diiipllooomatic areeenaa the blllaaaacccckkk has been basically ignored, and I mean on a world wiiiide level. My book addresses this problem and attempts, if I may say so . . . to provide some viable answers. My book is fourteeeeennnn hundred pages long."

He took a sip of Perrier and stared down at me. His jaws were sagging about a foot and a half now.

"Joseph, is it?" I was wearing one of those Branson tour bus type nametags. "What, pray tell, is the subject matter of your latest effort?"

"I have talking cats."

My friend Steve Robinson dropped his glass as well as his little plate of cheese.

Yes indeed. I have had many great experiences in my day job as Joe Bonsall, thirty-year member of the Oak Ridge Boys. And I believe my mother is very proud of her little Joey from Philly.

But I'll tell you, being Joseph has certainly been a unique journey as well.

HALLOWEEN

When my granddaughter was just three years old, she was coming over to our house on Halloween around 6 p.m. to show off her princess costume.

Well, Old Pop Pop here dug out his death costume. Full black robes, a huge skull head with red eyes that blinked on and off, and that big scythe. I dressed up and stood in the driveway like a statue as my daughter Sabrina and my little princess Breanne pulled into the driveway. Breanne got out of the car and gave me a good hard, apprehensive stare. Then all of a sudden my red eyes start to blink, and I turn to her and announce in a loud, creepy voice that . . . *I am the Paracles of Death and I have come to eat your nose! Bwahahahahaha.!!!*

Well, Princess Bre started to scream and run down the street in a fit of pure horror. Bottom line, I was in the doghouse with my wife Mary and my daughter Sabrina for a long time after that.

"She is just three years old! *What* is wrong with you???" (Very much paraphrased.)

Breanne would not talk to me for weeks. What I thought was funny may have scarred her forever, but the other night as I watched her play her Wii drums with *Journey* on rock band, while eating Fritos and talking on her cell phone . . . well, it would seem that she survived her encounter with the Paracles of Death!

Bwahahahahaha!!!

A LAZY MOON

There is a lazy moon just above the horizon. Beyond a quarter, and not quite a half. No one ever refers to a third of a moon do they? Anyhow, it is resting on its side, kind of like a rocker on a rocking chair. It has a pale yellow glow around it that isn't bright enough to obliterate the stars that are just hanging there all over the rest of the sky. They almost seem as if they are singing very quietly. Singing only to me.

The night is clear and the air is crisp. Except for a slight wind, there is not one discernible sound of any kind.

I saw twelve deer sleeping in the pasture behind the upper barn just a while ago while walking. My lamp lit them up, and I immediately turned and walked in another direction so as not to bother them. I sit on my front porch now in the darkness and stare at that lazy moon. It is rising up even farther now and growing smaller and brighter.

I can't see the deer from this vantage point, and yet I am somehow comforted in knowing they are there.

It is like you, Mom. I can't see you anymore, and yet . . . I know that you are there.

Can you see all this, my sweet Mother? It is a long way from the streets that we called home where the constant glare of a thousand lights hid all of this from our view.

We never shared one night that was ever this quiet. No . . . not one.

Do you see it, Mom? Do you? How does it look from that place where all is so beautiful?

Someday . . . we will know.

Someday . . . we will know.

Goodnight . . . I love you.

MY BIRTHDAY

May 18, 2003

Today we said goodbye to a saint. Oh, Valerie June Carter Cash would recoil and wave off such a thought. But in all honesty, this was a very special woman. She will be severely missed by not only Johnny Cash and the rest of her remaining family, but by all of us who existed on the periphery of her life.

Her friends and fans feel the emptiness today. That void is now filled only with the memory of her.

June loved the Oak Ridge Boys. She always called us her "babies."

Singing "Loving God, Loving Each Other," the wonderful Bill and Gloria Gaither song, while the Man in Black wept and waved to us is a memory that will last forever. Much like the memory of a sturdier Johnny Cash sitting on the front row of another funeral years ago, while the Oak Ridge Boys sang a Garland Craft song, "That's Just Like Jesus." The used temple that rested in the coffin on that day years ago had belonged to Momma Maybelle Carter, June's mother.

I can just imagine the reunion in Glory. June, her sisters, and Mother, all playing and singing again for the angels.

In a perfect world, John R. Cash does not say goodbye to June Carter; however, as we have all come to learn, this world is not a perfect place. Someday though, we will all witness perfection when the great choir gathers on that heavenly shore to sing for all eternity. There will be a lot of old friends in that choir and I plan to be right there among them singing my heart out.

"Loving God, Loving Each Other!"

This is not the first time I have said goodbye to a friend on my birthday. Our long time bus driver, Harley Pinkerman, also left us five years ago. Five years . . . hard to imagine.

So little Joey from Philly is now fifty-five years old. How about that!

When the funeral was over, I headed out to my farm. This place has become my refuge over and over again for the last five years. I always feel close to God while I am here in this holler that rests on the Kentucky-Tennessee line.

I took a ride alone on my John Deere Gator just before dusk. I saw a momma turkey protecting her eight little fuzzy babies who were struggling to keep up with her. I saw a beautiful doe seemingly all alone, but I knew she was guarding a newborn fawn, so I went the other way not wanting to disturb or alarm her.

The goldfinch and the summer tanagers were flitting along the fencerows, along with the chickadees and eastern bluebirds. I thought it rather early in the season for them to be here.

I park a while by the creek and listen. The previous storms have provided some strength to its ebb and flow, and the sounds of the rushing waters are very soothing. I stay a while and just listen.

Darkness falls, and as is usual for May, the night is filled with a ka-zillion lightning bugs blinking away as if they were a part of some fantasy movie. I almost expect a Hobbit to pop up and start talking to me.

Back at the cabin I sit on the front porch and continue to watch and listen to the show. All the barn swallows who share my home are roosting just above me and tolerating my presence. Two by two, one in the nest sitting on her eggs and the other just outside on guard. I counted fourteen pairs of swallows in the eaves and could not help laughing as I realized how many more will be buzzing by my head next month at this time. Come fall, before they decide to head on off to Capistrano or somewhere, there will be about 160 of them.

I go inside. Mary has made a nice meal and poured me a glass of my favorite Duckhorn Vineyards Cabernet. On ESPN the Phillies are even beating the Astros. Not bad.

Time to turn in, but first the message light on the phone is blinking.

I realize that I have been somewhat out of pocket on this birthday, and I see that I have missed several calls. My sister singing "Happy Birthday" at the top of her lungs (wonderful). My daughter Jen singing it like Elvis (hysterical). My daughter Sabrina and the grandkids singing "Happy Birthday to Pop Pop, Cha Cha Cha" (so sweet)! And then a call from my friend Duane Allen.

"Hey man, just wanted to tell you, that was one of the hardest things we ever had to do today, and I was so proud of all my singing partners. I was honored to be an Oak. When Johnny wept during our song, I near lost it, and I could tell you did too. Looks like your birthday got a little lost today, and I just wanted you to know how much I love you. Perhaps out there at the farm a few pieces will fall in place that will add up to a happy birthday. Good night, Yosef . . . see you at leaving time!"

"Coming to bed, hon?" Mary asks.

A few pieces have fallen in place for sure. Goodnight, June Carter Cash. One of your "babies" is having a very happy birthday!

Joe with Luke and Bre   *Photo courtesy of Joe Bonsall*

THE SUSHI IN ME

I have a deep passion for sushi. It all started in the early eighties when William Lee Golden had me try some raw tuna, sashimi style. I just fell in love with it. I could eat sushi every day, I think. Maguro tuna is still my favorite, but I also love salmon and yellowtail. I may grow a set of gills if I am not careful.

So with that thought in mind I give you this piece of total silliness called "The Sushi in Me." Sing it to the tune of Tim McGraw's "The Cowboy in Me." Ha ha!

So tune a fish, then . . . go tune a banjo . . . please!

The Sushi in Me
By Tuna Boy (sorry, Tim)

I always have some chop stix in my hand
A sushi bar is a place I understand
I even comprehend some Japanese
I guess that's just the sushi . . . in me

I realize that my hands smell just like fish
There's always some wasabe on my breath
I wash it down with a cup of hot green tea
I guess that's just the sushi . . . in me

(Bridge)

A tuna roll, a bowl of rice
A crunchy shrimp, a hint of spice
Fresh water eel or salmon raw
Some yellowtail or albacore
A sushi bar in every town would be okay, you see
I guess that's just the sushi . . . in me

(Repeat Bridge)

A tuna roll a bowl of rice
A crunchy shrimp, a hint of spice
Fresh water eel or salmon raw
Some yellowtail or albacore
A sushi bar in every town would be okay, you see
I guess that's just the sushi . . . in me

I always try to sample something new
I guess there's some things even I won't do
Octopus or fish eggs I won't eat
I guess that's just the sushi . . . in me.
Tuna Boy's a name that I am called
There may be a little sushi . . . in us all

Words and music by Joseph S. Bonsall.
Copyright © 2003 B's in the Trees Music (ASCAP).
Administered by Gaither Copyright Management.

WAITING ON THE MOON

September 12, 2003, 10 p.m.

By now the whole wide world knows that John R. Cash passed away in the early hours on this beautiful September day. I was awakened at 6 a.m. in my bunk on our tour bus by our road manager, Timmer Ground, who had just been awakened by a call from good friend, radio talk show host, and author Phil Valentine. The bus was parked right by our office and had probably pulled in around 4 a.m. or so.

The Oak Ridge Boys had performed last night at a fair in Abington Virginia, and we would now be home for two days before heading down to Jacksonville, Florida, for Sunday. William and Richard had already awakened and headed for the house, and Duane Allen was sitting quietly and sadly in the front of the bus watching a multitude of people reflecting on the life of the Man in Black. There was Johnny singing, looking young and vibrant. There he was looking frail and sickly. A constant montage of John and June would play all day on radio and television, and for me . . . I chose solitude.

Much like when my Mom and Dad and even June Carter passed on to Glory, I went to my farm in the country alone to reflect, remember, and pray. I would also try to get some work done.

I spent most of this day cutting grass on a small John Deere tractor pulling a six-foot Woods finishing mower. I toiled at this for six hours and for the most part I just enjoyed the beauty of the day. It was around eighty degrees or so and the sun was shining and I was trying to follow my own philosophy of celebrating life. I had spent an hour with my grandchildren and daughter Sabrina before I came out to the country, and being with them was very healing. My Mary was knee deep in her

Friday cleaning day and urged me to go on out to the farm. She usually knows what I need, and besides, I am always in the way at home on Fridays anyway!

I called her at 5:30 p.m. to advise her that I was getting the big tractor out and planned to get a start on cutting a field I call Cockle Burr Hill for obvious reasons. I told her I would cut until well after dark, probably until the moon came up.

This may sound silly, but to me, driving a tractor at night reminds me of my boating days. For about ten years we owned a forty-foot Chris Craft express cruiser, and my favorite thing to do was to pilot that thing down the Cumberland River late at night. We'd take a day trip from Hendersonville's Old Hickory Lake, though the lock, and down the river to downtown Nashville. We would dock in town and go out for a nice dinner, and then Mary would go to the cabin and watch TV or go to bed, and I would drive another three or four hours, usually to a place called Gowers Island near Ashland City and drop anchor.

Waking up there was wonderful, but I still dream about sitting in the flybridge and gunning those twin Volvo Penta engines to a nice cruising speed down the river on a cool fall night. Passing barges, the wind in my face, drinking hot chocolate handed to me in my captain's cup from my first and only mate down below.

Believe me, the tractor ride late at night feels exactly the same!

I watch a beautiful sunset. A painted sky, all purple and red. It begins to darken. I stop and put another five gallons of co-op red dye diesel fuel in the tank. I crank it up and ride some more. The big ten-foot rotary cutter is working well, and I am literally assassinating cockle burrs.

Then it starts to hit me hard. Johnny is gone. Not a surprise, really. Why, the last time I saw him at June's funeral I didn't think he would last a day, but this is Johnny Cash. Never underestimate this man. Was it Bono of the rock group U-2 who said, "Every man, knows deep in his heart that compared to Johnny Cash he is a sissy"?

Indeed! I can count on one hand the people that I have ever met who actually gave me a chill when they entered the room. I met Elvis and John Wayne just one time, and that was a thrill. Seeing Gregory Peck in a restaurant once in Vegas was cool. Meeting Gene Autry and Roy Rogers was pretty darn cool too, but I *knew* Johnny Cash. I had performed with him, backed him up on several records, sang at his wife, June's, funeral as well his mother-in-law's, Momma Maybelle Carter. We have been to his house. I have even run into him at Eckerd Drug Store, for crying out loud, yet still, a chill.

"Whoa man . . . there he is!"

That charisma, that voice, that magic, that charm, that confidence, the talent, the boyish grin—yes, what a smile! When I ran into him one day and he hugged me, I actually cried. I couldn't help it!

I asked, "How are you, John?"

He threw his head back as if onstage and said, "The demons keep nipping at my heels, Joe, but God is good, and if I can just keep on trusting him to help me, I'll be just fine."

Yes, John R. Cash had his demons, but he had two saviors. He was married to one of them, and the other now holds them both in His everlasting arms.

It is 9 p.m., and I am tired of riding and cutting and thinking, but I don't want to get off this hill until the moon comes up. I have been riding in circles, looking at Mars and waiting on the moon. The hollar below is filling with a misty fog. From the top of this hill I can't even see my house down there. I stop and shut it all down. It is so quiet.

I can't help but feel a bit depressed. So much death everywhere the last few years. Mommy and Daddy. I think of Rosanne and the other Cash kids. They lost their mother and father in the same year as well. Instant orphans. Been there. Still there! So many are gone who were here not long ago.

What is that? The bright yellow light behind the tree line appears so suddenly that I must admit it scares me. For a moment I think that God had sent an angel, and I am not sure that He didn't. However, now I see that this light comes from the moon that is just beginning to rise.

Wow . . . it's coming up huge! Not quite as full as two nights ago, or even last night. There is a small chip off the old block, but still . . . it is beautiful. Well worth the wait. As it ascends into the misty sky I find myself wishing that everyone I love could be sitting right here with me.

Sitting on top of Cockle Burr Hill, thinking of the Man in Black and waiting on the moon . . .

I feel better now.

Good night, John.

WHAT? HUH?

One day when my granddaughter, Breanne, was around three or maybe four years old, she was going on and on to Mom Mom about a story that had appeared magically inside her head. At one point Mary exclaimed, "Oh Bre, you are pulling my leg!"

A puzzled Breanne answered, "I am not pulling your leg, Mom Mom!"

How could she possibly have known what that phrase meant? She was not pulling Mary's leg, and what in the world did that have to do with her story about a princess and the busy birds?

Then there was the Mary-grandson day. Luke was alarmed by the fact that every single time he came to visit us our kitty Sally Ann would hide under the bed. Mom Mom explained that it had nothing to do with him. It was just that Sally Ann was afraid of her own shadow.

It took about an hour for a bewildered little boy to ask, "Mom Mom, just what does Sally Ann's shadow look like?"

When my daughter Jennifer was a little girl, my sister, Nancy, once warned her to not throw the baby out with the bathwater. This may have scarred her for life!

Back in time now to little Joey.

When I was born in Philadelphia way back in 1948, I came into the world via a C-section. I also arrived with a case of jaundice. I was as yellow as a Crayola crayon, and from what I heard later on, my father fainted dead away when he beheld his newly born, yellowish son.

My mother was never great with words, so during childhood when I would hear the adults talking to each other, I used to get pretty freaked out by some of the things they would say. I was actually a very sickly little boy who constantly battled bronchial asthma, and I always figured it was because I had to be "cut out," or that I was born with "the jaundice." Thanks, Mom! I am now sixty-one years old, and I am still obviously freaking out a bit over it!

"Yes, son, I was very sick when I had you. They had to cut you out, and they had to take my gall bladder too!"

Gees . . . sorry, Mother!

A few years later they had to cut my sister out as well!

My mother used to blame us both for her "hesions." To this day I do not know what that is. Nancy has no idea either. All we know was that Mommy had "the hesions" and it was our fault. It was a lot like, "Your Uncle Roy just called. He has the shingles!" Ohhhhhhhh.

When I was four I developed a persistent sore throat. After a visit with our family doctor I was told that I would have to go into the hospital. "They will put you under, and then take out your tonsils and adenoids!"

Adenoids? My adenoids???

I was four years old, and in the days leading up to my being put "under," I was a basket case. I might have just as well had to walk the Green Mile to the electric chair or walk the plank. For a moment, though, let us dwell on the plank.

One has to wonder about the logistics. Did a pirate ship actually come with a plank?

"Captain Blackbeard, where on the ship's perimeter would you like the new plank to be built, sir?'

Or did they have to put it up every time it was to be walked? Was somebody onboard in charge of the plank?

"Argh, where did I put that thing?"

All of this was scary stuff when I was a kid. Especially . . . *the chair!* My father always talked about the chair.

"Yes son he's going to *the chair!* You know if you kill a man, they give you *the chair!* They sit you right down on that thing, strap you in, and then they electrocute ya! People actually burn to a crisp in *the chair!"*

I'll tell you, Dracula or the Wolf Man had nothing on the chair! Of course, there was the gas chamber, which was also pretty darn creepy because they "gas ya to death!!" I think I would have preferred walking the plank to either of those!

I remember a school trip in sixth grade when the whole class from the John H. Webster Elementary was taken for a visit to a closed up, decayed prison. Whoever came up with that idea?

As I remember, the boys got a much bigger kick out of seeing old cells with grimy wire beds, pee-stained mattresses, and broken toilets than the girls ever did. But when they actually showed the class *the chair,* school was out for little Joey!

That thing was just as creepy as I thought it might be, and with spider webs hanging all over it and with the smell of the dank and damp room and . . . well, you get the picture. I had nightmares for about three years and promised God with all of my heart that I would *never . . . ever . . .* kill anyone.

Some things were not as scary. How about this?

"Joey, your father will look after you tonight. I have to go work at the polls."

"Dad? What are the polls?"

"Someplace where your mother volunteers to work. People vote there. Get me a beer!"

Oh, I understand now. Thanks, Dad. Huh?

My father could really be inspiring. On most mornings after too much beer and cigarettes the night before, there he would be, standing over the toilet coughing and gagging and making the worse sounds a kid could imagine.

I stood in the doorway of the bathroom one day and watched. He actually had a lit-up Winston in one hand as he almost tossed a lung against the wall. He turned to me and pointed the cigarette at my face and growled, "If I ever see you smoking one of these things, I swear I will shove it up your little can—lit end first!!"

No wonder I never smoked. I mean *who* would want *that?* Thanks again, Dad!

There are so many phrases we hear as children and do not understand. Things like, "Your eyes are bigger than your stomach." Huh? "That thing will put your eye out." What? "Look with your eyes not with your hands." Hah?? "It is raining cats and dogs outside." Amazing!

So many of these confusing phrases exist to this day, but in my childhood there were a few different ones.

"Your father just got fired." Oh, my God!

"Boy, one day you will come to realize that *that* thing is more than just to pee with." It is?

"Mom, why did Daddy come home from work all bloody?"

"They had a wildcat strike, and your father crossed the picket line."

Oh, okay . . . thanks, Mom. I totally understand. Happy you cleared that up for me!

"Mommy, why did my friend Curtis have to die?"

"His heart was bad and it just exploded, honey. He was coming home from school, and it just went boom!"

Holy cow—that would be worse than *the chair!*

AMERICA

GUN STORIES

A nyone who has read my book, *G.I. Joe and Lillie,* can easily attest to the fact that I am a student of World War II. It was that time in history when many of our parents and grandparents rose up high above themselves. They accomplished extraordinary things to save America from the tyranny of Nazism and totalitarianism, both of which threatened our very freedom. Our young men and women went where they were sent. They fought and bled and died in the fields and on the shores of Europe as well as the islands and oceans of the Pacific.

The sacrifices made and the price that was paid by so many must never be forgotten. It is why I wrote a book and a song about the lives of my parents, PFC Joseph S. Bonsall, Sr. and Cpl. Lillie M. Collins Bonsall. In telling the story of one couple whose lives were forever shaped by the events of this incredible war, I was honoring and remembering so many just like them—those who gave so much of themselves and fought so that I could sit here today at an antique desk, using a modern MacBook Pro laptop to write anything that I want to write without fear of retribution. I pray this is always the case in America, and I am thankful to the many brave men and women who are still fighting around the world for this same freedom!

The enemy may be a bit different in nature in this modern age than it was in my parents' time, but there are enemies nonetheless, and they must be defeated on every front. I am thankful to God that, like G. I. Joe and Lillie, our young men and women in the service are still ready and willing—and more able then ever before—to get the job done. We must pray for them every single day.

But back to WWII. This is the story of two different guns from that era. Two guns that were there on D-Day. Two guns that now rest deep inside my safe have influenced my life on many levels, and I cannot pick one up and hold it without weeping like a child.

Here is the why!

The M-1 Garand

My father and those brave young men who surrounded him on June 6, 1944, carried an M-1 Garand. Joe Bonsall, Sr., had one slung over his shoulder when he hit the beach code-named Utah on that Day of Days. He was just nineteen years old. After fifty days of battle, he was hit hard near Saint Lo, France, when German bullets tore through his body as he singlehandedly rescued his platoon from Nazi machine-gun nests. His Bronze Star, Silver Star, and clustered Purple Heart are the reason why he and his Lillie rest in Arlington today.

The book about their lives garnered many friends for your author. Many of these friends have become unforgettable. One friend, Eddie Polk, lives in Slidell, Louisiana, and makes his living by taking veterans on battlefield tours around the world. He knows hundreds of wonderful old vets from just about everywhere, and I think he has bought a copy of *G.I. Joe and Lillie* for all of them.

Eddie loved my little book, and we corresponded by e-mail for years. One day the Oak Ridge Boys were playing a date outside of New Orleans, and I arranged to meet him at last. We spent a whole day together, talking about the war and veterans and battles and battlefields. We even toured the D Day museum together. We laughed and we cried and we ate dinner, and then we wept some more as each of us shared stories.

That night after the show Eddie hugged me and told me he would like to do something special for me. Knowing Eddie had contacts all around the world, I sheepishly asked him if there was any way he could find a Garand, the most storied rifle of WWII. I told him I would pay whatever price was required for the M-1.

He assured me that he could find one and that there would be no charge at all. I hate to say it, but I wept again right there in the parking lot. About six months later Eddie called and said he had the gun and wanted to know where to ship it. By law, he had to ship it to a local gun store, so I arranged to have it shipped to a place in Gallatin, Tennessee. He said it should arrive there within a week.

Well, I hit the road with the Oaks for about a ten-day trip, and somewhere in the middle of the tour I received a call from the gun store. The Garand was there. I told the proprietor that I would be back home in just a few days and would pick it up on Thursday around noon.

The day arrived. I was home and all unpacked and excited. I drove to the gun store in Gallatin and could not believe there was no place to park. I had to drive two more blocks to park my car. I walked back to the store and, much to my surprise, the place was packed. There must have been twenty or more old men stuffed into this little place. There on the counter was a long cardboard container wrapped in shipping tape and labels and such. The man behind the counter was in tears.

"We have been waiting for you," he said. "No way would we have opened this here box until you got here."

Then it hit me. These old men were all veterans, and they had gathered here to see and touch an M-1 Garand rifle.

I said, "Well, crack that thing open!"

The gun was beautiful. The gun was immaculate! The gun was like my daddy's gun! The gun represented history!

The Garand was passed all around the store. Old men held it close to their hearts. Old men wept like children. Old men who had been there in the forties held the Garand and remembered when they had held one that was, oh, so similar. Stories began to emerge and more men wept. I wept right along with them.

The owner of the store gave me two boxes of 30-06 shells and instructed me how to safely load and unload a Garand. "Do this wrong and you could lose a finger!" he said as many in the room laughed. One old guy held up his hand to expose two fingers missing. That received a huge laugh.

I thought about how hard it might be to pick a banjo without a finger, so I paid strict attention to the lesson. After several hours, we gently put the Garand back in the box. A man stepped forward and gave me two magazines that he had kept since the war. "Use these when you fire that thing!" he said as he hugged me and held on to me for a bit.

He backed away and said, "Shoot that gun, son, so you will know how your daddy felt when *he* shot one. Then put it up in a safe place.

That gun has probably been to hell and back, just like us, just like your father. Take care of it!"

I walked back to my truck carrying a cardboard box loaded with history. I have since shot and cleaned my M-1 Garand. Just like my daddy did in 1944. Just like these old Tennessee veterans did. The gun is in a safe place.

Thanks, Daddy!! Thank you, Eddie Polk!

The Incredible Journey of One U.S. Army-issued 45-Caliber Semi-automatic Sidearm

My best friend outside of my group of singing partners is Darrell Bowling, a former *semper fi* Marine and a master trooper in the Virginia State Patrol. His son, Cpl. Jonathon W. Bowling, USMC, made the ultimate sacrifice in Iraq on January 26, 2005, when a rocket-propelled grenade hit the vehicle in which he was riding. Four Marines died for our freedom on that day, including Darrell's boy, Jon. I wear a black bracelet on my right arm in honor of his memory. I always will!

Well, a year or so back, Darrell came to see me and brought a gun case with him. He proceeded to tell me a story about an old veteran neighbor of his who was a part of the first wave of attack on the bloody beach codenamed Omaha on D-Day. The same moments my dad was trying to stay alive on Utah beach, this man ran down the ramp of his Higgins Landing Craft and found himself swimming, and then fighting, his way across Omaha beach and beyond. The first story I heard was that he found this army-issued 45-caliber sidearm in the sand. After having lost his own gun in the water, he was darned glad to have it.

The soldier survived the war, and when he came home to be discharged back into the United States, he was ordered to turn in his firearms. He presented the sidearm he had carried throughout the European Theater of Operations and was told that the paperwork on a "found gun" was too much of a task to deal with. "Throw the thing in the ocean or put it back in your pack, I do not care! Now move on, soldier."

He placed the gun in his pack and kept it until the day he died. He wanted a good man to have it, so he chose to give it to a dear friend, whom he had loved since the man was a young boy, a decorated policeman named Darrell Bowling, who would one day pass the gun on to his son, another young policeman named Jonathon Bowling.

This storied little gun that had been found on Omaha Beach on June 6, 1944, became Jon's favorite. He would shoot and clean it on a regular basis and, when the time came to join the Marines and serve his country, young Jonathan put the gun back in his father's care and asked him to watch after it until he returned home.

Darrell held on to his son's gun for many years, and then he gave it me. On the day he came to visit, he told me the story of the gun, and then opened the case. What a beautiful gun. Just holding it in my hand gave me a sense of the men who owned it. Through eyes full of tears, Darrell said two words that I hear every time I look at this gun. "It's yours."

I told Darrell I was not worthy to have this gun, and that he should have it. This tough old Marine and state cop, who had given his only son, told me that our friendship has meant the world to him and that the Oak Ridge Boys had helped him get through some tough times. Besides that, he said, "Jon would want you to have it."

Two more years passed before Darrell told me the rest of the story. With Darrell's permission I would like to use part of a note that he sent to me. His words are better than mine on this account.

I spent some time with some veterans today. We honored Jon and began to talk about our local heroes who had gone through hell and were now gone. We honored my son. I even drove Jon's truck on this day.

As I went back to Jon's little truck, my mind wandered to another time and another story that I never have quite been able to get out to you and speak of. Maybe on this keyboard, and away on my own without you looking at me, I can.

I had just turned 13 and would rise each morning to deliver *The Roanoke Times* around town. Each morning Richard would have me some kind of little treat to eat as I stopped by on my route with my bicycle. This morning, he did not walk out to me and was just sitting in his carport. So, not knowing any better, I just went right on up to him. He sat there and he was crying, and in his lap was a 45-cal. auto. A beautiful Gun, and I am sure that he noticed my boyish stare. It was June 6th.

I asked him what was wrong and he just said, that he was just remembering the Day. He told me about what had happened on that day so many years ago. As he spoke he was quiet in his speech and reverend in his manners. I sat down and he shared with a little boy, memories that bring tears to my eyes even now.

He was on his way to shore in a landing craft, they were all praying and observing the death and destruction as they neared the beach. Then an artillery shell hit them and Richard woke up in the water floating. Most of the ones around him were floating just like him, except lifeless. They were two far out in way too deep of water. Many drowned from the weight of their gear. When he woke up, his pack and rifle were gone. He started swimming for shore, as his ship was way too far away. As he got closer to shore the hail of bullets became thicker and so did the bodies. There were others all around him so it was packed as they waited their turn to get to shore. At some point he noticed a man trying to hold his head above water and in his right hand was a .45 held high above his head to keep it out of the water. When he got over to him, it became apparent that the man was gravely wounded. Richard said he was having trouble keeping afloat and his intestines were swimming around in the water in front on him. He grabbed him, and started swimming with him. Richard said the man (whom he had never seen and did not know) asked him to get him to shore saying, "I have to make it to shore, I have to know that I got there, I have to!"

They did eventually get there and as he dragged him onto the beach he saw just how bad the Man was wounded. He said the Man thanked him as he was holding his parts with his left hand while all the time holding that .45 up high. He told Richard to take it, as he would no longer need it. Richard stayed with him and said as bad as it was and noisy as it was, he heard nothing and saw nothing as he looked into the man's eyes. The Man then hollered at him to just go . . . when he came to his senses the bullets were striking all around him. He said as he ran off he looked back at the Man who had given him the Auto, and the Man was holding his arm up and shouting at him " Keep it dry, keep it dry . . . "

Tears rolled down his face as he looked down at the gun, and he said," I never knew the man but this gun saved my life on so many occasions. I have no idea of how many I had to kill with this gun . . . but it was either me or them." He told me " so that's why I am sitting here with this thing and thinking about the man who gave it to me and the men whose lives I have taken Today, Darrell, I am thinking and praying for them all! I guess that is why today still means so much to me."

I went by his home often just to visit over the years and a few weeks before he died he summoned me to the hospital. Richard was loosing his long battle with Cancer. When I went into the room, his wife got out a small green bag out of her pocket book and laid it on his chest and hugged me and left the room. Richard (always smiling) asked me how I was doing. He chatted for a while about things and he told me that everything would be just fine. He handed me the green bag and said " Here." In it was the .45! He said he had tried to turn it in upon coming home, but the supply Sgt had such a fit about all the paper work since it was not supposed to be with him, that he just put it in his 1st aide green bag and brought it home.

I first told him that I could not take it, but he stopped me. He said, "I have no son, but you, Darrell. You have heart, something few have now, and I want you to have it. Some day when you run across someone else who has heart, give it to them and think of me."

I don't know, but it was like he knew so much more than I did at that time. Really as I think about it, I guess he did. As I looked back at him lying there in the bed, Richard raised his right arm and smiled and said, "Keep it dry, keep it dry." I never saw Richard again until the day I helped carry him to his grave.

So . . . now you know the rest of the story that I was smiling about, when I got to Jonathan's pickup. I have had the very real pleasure of placing that weapon into the hands of two people that have had very much heart. My own son and now you!

Keep it dry Joe; keep it dry.

Such an honor! *Such* an honor!
The two guns rest side by side in my safe. The M-1 Garand as well as the storied U.S. Army-issue 45-caliber semiautomatic

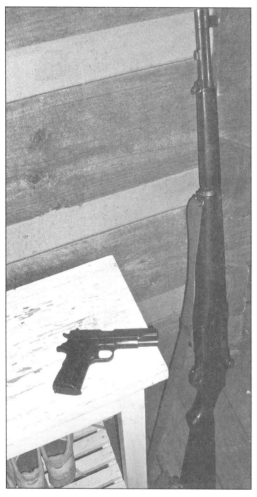

sidearm. Two guns that have been to hell and back! I have fired them both. I have cleaned them, and I have wept over them time and again.

Most of all . . . I have kept them dry!

Addendum

My dear friend and brother Darrell Bowling had a habit of putting his initials upon anything that was meaningful to him. He habitually wrote three letters, and his son seemed to take up the same custom as his dad. Jon would write J. W. B. on just about everything he owned, and his dad always got quite the kick out of that. After Darrell made the heartfelt decision to give the gun to your author, he found himself sitting down one night and gathering up the stuff that he would send with it. He had a new case for the gun and had also added the tiny green U.S. Army first-aid bag the old veteran had given him.

His son had bought a much newer leather holster in which to carry the gun. Darrell removed the .45 from the holster and examined it closely. There on the inside of the holster, written in black ink, were his son's familiar initials except for one thing. For the first time that Darrell could ever remember, his son left out the middle character. There were only the two letters: J. B. It was if his young Marine son was agreeing with him that it was okay to give the .45 to Joe Bonsall!

Author note: This commentary was written in the Garth Mansion in Hannibal, Missouri, on August 22, 2009, in the bedroom where Mark Twain once slept. Thank you, Mister Clemens!

VETERANS

There is always something special for me and all of the Oak Ridge Boys to do on Veterans Day and the days that lead up to the celebration. Over the years we have taken part in many events that honor those who have served and paid the price for the freedoms we enjoy on a daily basis in this great United States of America.

As a member of a group that has always honored our heroes, and the author of the book *G.I. Joe and Lillie,* I have been provided with a full slate of good things to do. That suits all of us just fine. From huge celebrations in our nation's capitol to a small speech on the steps of a bank in Macon County, Tennessee, as a group or as individuals, we always take time to honor our veterans.

For instance, this year we were in Branson, Missouri, on Veterans Day, and that town goes all out to honor those who have served in every war. We honored vets at every show and sang the national anthem at two huge events. One was a city-wide welcome for veterans, and the other was a huge birthday celebration for the U.S. Marine Corps.

Lt. Col. Oliver North was the speaker at the Marine Corps event, and we were moved as we watched young Marines, who are fighting today, being honored by old Marines. Together they honored the Corps. *Semper fidelis!*

There was an empty table for one adorned in black ribbon, which paid tribute to the fallen leathernecks who were not there in body, but in spirit. There was a Purple Heart on the table, as well as a set of dog tags with no name. I thought of young men like Jon Bowling of Virginia and so many just like him who paid the ultimate cost for you and me. It was all very moving.

One day I was fortunate enough to spend an entire afternoon in Branson at a place the vets call the day room. Hundreds gather there to tell stories and eat cookies, and many sit in a circle and pick bluegrass music. Ole Ban-Joey found himself right there in the pickin' circle trying not to get in the way of the better players with my half-baked banjo playing. But, overall, I played pretty well and had a blast. We picked and laughed and cried some as well. In honor of my being a part of their day, they put a big picture of my parents on the honor wall, and I was moved beyond words at the gesture.

Mommy and Daddy have been gone for many years now, and they would be happy, I am sure, to know that their son Joey has been a part of so many events like this. Because of my book and song, I have been invited over and over to many such events over the years, and I try to make as many as possible. I often find myself behind a podium speaking to veterans groups or visiting old warriors and listening to their stories.

Now, I must be honest and admit to you that sometimes this is very hard for me, and I will tell you why. In my parents' final years they lived in the Southeastern Pennsylvania Veterans Center. Daddy was weak from decades of disability, and Mommy's battle with diabetes made it impossible for her to give him the care he needed. So they moved to what my mom called the Soldiers Home, where she would be surrounded with veterans like her and Daddy. I will tell you, they were treated like gold in that place. Their every need was met with a love and respect that doesn't always exist in a care facility.

Nevertheless, it broke my heart to see them there! I always left that place feeling thankful, and yet so very dark inside. Many of us have to deal with a parent or a grandparent who must have the kind of care they can no longer receive at home, and for everyone who has ever seen their loved ones enter a retirement home of any kind, there is that deep, knowing reality that washes over you like a tidal wave. This is the last stop. The final exit. It is not an easy road.

A few years ago, while visiting a veterans' home in California, I was so overcome with emotion I had to leave early. It was just one time I could not take it. The sights, the sounds, and the smells all reminded me of my father lying in bed with a blanket pulled up over his head wishing he were somewhere else. But, of course, when I get really down like this, it is thoughts of my mother that bail me out and lift my spirits back up to where they should be. I can just hear her thanking me for taking the time to honor those who have fought. She loved them all—and so do I!

She was the most positive person on the face of this earth. She could make apple pie out of any pile of negativity that came down the pike. She loved God and she loved America. She was also a very funny woman. So on a lighter note, I share this little story.

Lillie went on and on to me on the phone one day about this little hairdresser girl who would drive up from Royersford, Pennsylvania, and do her hair for free. It seemed that there were six female vets living there at the time, and on a Saturday morning this young lady would cut and style all their hair, which was very sweet of her to do.

My mom just adored her. Well, I took a trip up North to visit them, and as I sat there with her in the room, Mommy advised me that she had set up a personal meet and greet with me and the other ladies who resided at SEPVC. I, of course, agreed. I really had no choice in the matter. Daddy had been gone for several months at this point in time.

Well, I am pushing Mommy down the hall on the way to a recreation room of sorts, and looking down at her hair, I had to choke back a laugh. The young hairdresser had this rounded-off tight-curl thing going that was really quite humorous. Now, Mommy did not have a ton of hair anymore, but what she had going for her was a new look for certain. Up to that point I had never seen anything quite like it. It was sort of a helmet, but more like an upside down bowl. It was not locked into place either. It seemed to actually move around a bit, as if it had a life of its own. Not movement per se. It sort of breathed on its own. I have no real words to describe it.

So we enter the room, and there are five other old women waiting for us. Three were in wheelchairs, one was sitting on a couch, and the other was standing. They all had the same exact living, breathing helmet on their heads. It took all the self-control I could muster to not roll around the floor. It was just downright funny.

After I got over the matching hairdos, however, I sat and listened as I always do. For, as usual, each one had a story to tell. These ladies seemed very happy that they had someone with whom to share a little piece of their journey, and I was downright thrilled to be listening. All of these girls were alone. Like Mommy, their husbands were now at rest. Their remains were interred beneath a white stone on a green field, and very soon they would be right there with them.

I wish I had taken notes. I could have written a book on each one of them. I have always believed that the success of *G.I. Joe and Lillie* is in the line "An American love story not unlike a lot of others," for so many have lived a similar story. I find that when men open up about these things, which they rarely do, they talk about the battles and their buddies. It would seem that older veteran women talk more about their love for their men than they ever talk about themselves.

They all wept as they remembered their husband's battle scars and, on every level, displayed their undisputed love for him, no matter what he may have ever done wrong. "It was the war that made him act that way," and they would stand by him through thick and thin. It was a common mantra and was quite inspiring for certain.

One time in South Dakota I witnessed a meeting of two old men who were in the same division, fought the same battles, and had never met until that moment. These old soldiers blocked out their families, and the Oak Ridge Boys, who were in the room, connected on a level that anyone who has not experienced combat could never dream about. Men who had never spoken a word about the experience opened up to each other. Remember this? Remember that? It was magical and very moving. I am so happy to have been there for that one. They laughed and they cried, and so did everyone else in the room.

The bottom line here is obvious to those of us who care. The price for freedom is always paid in blood. War after war . . . prices paid . . . sacrifices made. Today we still ask our young men and women to protect and to serve America, and they do just that. They always have!

No matter what your political or religious persuasion these days, you do need to love these kids. Hold them up in prayer and support them. For, as with all the veterans who have gone before them, they are the best of us!

Jesus knew all about this when He said there was no greater love than for one to lay down his life for a friend. He knew that the real price of freedom and redemption would have to be paid for in blood as well. He was willing to pay that price on a very personal level for each of us, and He suffered more pain and humiliation than anyone has ever gone through before or after. Personal level? Yes, very personal, because He did it for me. What can wash away my sin? Nothing but the blood of Jesus!

What our veterans have done is also very personal to your author. I believe their service and sacrifice is for me as well, and for all of us who love freedom. We just need to remember them once in a while, and when you get a chance, thank them for what they have done for us. On Veterans Day and on every day!

When I was little, my mom would take me down to the veterans' parade on Kensington Avenue. She would salute, and she would cry when the flag went by. In those days the old veterans would sell these little, red, poppy flowers to raise money for the local VFW posts, and Lillie would buy them from every single person who was selling them.

I asked, "Mom, what are you going to do with all of those?"

She said it did not matter what was done with them. "What matters is that you never forget what these veterans have done for this country! They are all like your father! They are heroes. I could never buy enough of these things!"

I have not forgotten, Mom!

Prices paid . . . sacrifices made.

God bless those who have served in the military, and God bless those who serve today. Bring them home safely to their loved ones

when the battle is over and help them to live with the pain they have experienced while fighting for our freedom here at home. I ask this in the name of Him who shed His blood and, in so doing, provided for us a new freedom and a life everlasting, Jesus Christ! Amen!

Photo courtesy of Joe Bonsall

A DAY ON THE EAGLE'S WING

The Oaks arrived in Salt Lake City early on the morning of July 28, 2003. We had played the Montana State Fair in Great Falls the previous night, and most everyone was still asleep in his bunk as we dropped anchor across from the Little America Hotel. Tonight we would sing at a private party held by the Skaggs Drug Store family. Then our Red, White and BluBlocker tour would head eastward.

I admit to being wide-awake when our driver Billy Smith shut the big engine down. In fact, I really didn't sleep very much throughout the night because I was so excited about the upcoming events.

After breakfast and a quick clean up, I would be heading to Ogden, Utah. After an hour signing copies of *G.I. Joe and Lillie* at a MediaPlay store, I would have a day on the Eagle's Wing! Ogden is the home of Hill Air Force Base as well as the Ogden Air Logistics Center. Hill AFB can boast of the famed 388th Fighter Wing and the 75th Air Base Wing.

I had been honored with an invitation to speak to the young men and woman in uniform who serve at Hill. The gathering was called a Commander's Call and would take place inside Hanger 37.

Several thousand were in attendance. The entire base command was there, along with young airmen and women and many civilian support workers. Special guests included about twenty old veterans, many with their wives. Veterans from all the services: Army, Marines, Navy and Air Force. Veterans of many battles, from Bataan to the Bulge, from Korea to Vietnam. The only living Medal of Honor winner in the State of Utah, Mr. George Whalen, was there. He was a hero at Iwo Jima.

This entire group gathered together for just one reason: to listen to me talk, an honor way beyond words and so hard for me to describe.

It was not only humbling, but in all honesty it was one of the greatest moments of my entire life. A part of me was scared to death, but I was prepared and ready to thank our nation's best for their service. I was ready to talk about America!

A huge flag hung behind me as I stood at the podium. I felt like General Patton. After the speech I presented each veteran as well as members of the Air Command with copies of *G.I. Joe and Lillie* and the Oaks' new patriotic CD, *Colors*. On behalf of New Leaf Press, I presented each of them with a signed and numbered *G.I. Joe and Lillie* collectible, suited for framing and containing a beautiful quote from the book about there being "no greater love than that of a soldier, one for the other."

While taking a picture with the old veterans, we all broke into a chorus of *Elvira*, as the young ones cheered. I spent a lot of time talking with these kids and taking pictures with them. They are the best of America, and I will always remember the way they treated me.

Then . . . *bonus time.* A reward. Colonel Charlie Lyon, the commander of the 388th FW, escorted me on a VIP tour of the base, which included not only seeing an F-16 up close and learning all about it, but actually sitting in the cockpit. (If General Yeager could see me now!)

I was privileged to sit in on an informative briefing, which concerned the base, its history, its logistical info, its planes, its air-support team, and its capabilities. If those who would harm us ever took a look at this film, they would be waving white flags and taking apart their weapons. "So sorry . . . big mistake . . . let's make peace . . . please don't come here. How about those Yankees and Braves?"

Unfortunately evil empires, dictators, and regimes of terror must be first shown—up close and personal—that messing with the United States is not a good move. Well, bring 'em on!

Then I spent time in a classroom, learning about an F-16 flight simulator. Why? Glad you asked. Old Tenor Boy here flew an F-16. Thankfully it was indeed simulated. I did well for a while. I took off out of Hill with no problem. I even did a roll or two and survived. Then the commander pulled up an enemy battleship that began firing at me. Hey, man, Nintendo was never like this! I was told to nose up, and then do a power dive at the ship, which was firing ordinance at me from the middle of the Great Salt Lake (which is impossible, haha!). I dove. I had the enemy in my sights and opened fire. BLAM. BLAM! I blew that ship to pieces. I was feeling good. Those around me cheered.

"Pull up! Pull up!" my instructor yelled.

Aw-oh. I couldn't do it. Can you say, "Hand basket?"

EH EH EH EH!!!

Yes, I crashed a twenty-seven-million-dollar F-16 directly into the Great Salt Lake. (This time I was glad General Yeager *wasn't* there.) Nevertheless, I am quite sure my mom and dad were proud of me today. I shared a little piece of them with America, and it was such an honor to have been able to do so.

Until the day my precious Savior takes me Home to meet with them once again, I will never forget that day—a day when a street kid from Philly got to spend a little bit of time on the Eagle's Wing.

Photo by Jon Mir

I wrote this piece in 2001, when we were in Broken Bow for the Windmill Festival for the first time. As I read over this little essay on Americana on June 12, 2003, I found myself once again sitting in the Gateway Motel in beautiful Broken Bow, Nebraska. They still had not built a Holiday Inn or even a newer mom and pop motel. In fact, not one single thing had changed since that first visit. No, not one! For some reason this brought me comfort.

BROKEN BOW, NEBRASKA

I hope the dear folks who reside in central Nebraska will forgive me for calling today's gig "the end of the universe" in a radio interview earlier.

The town we have spent a good part of the afternoon living in is actually Broken Bow, Nebraska. The gig is in Comstock, Nebraska, which is a good thirty miles from here.

We are leaving in an hour. Rascal Flatts' bus just pulled out of the Gateway Motel parking lot, where our bus is gently idling away the ninety-three-degree afternoon. Today it is Sarah Evans and Colin Raye who will share the Windmill stage with the Boys.

One is always leery of a motel whose rooms number one through twenty-five. I am in room number 16 at this moment. However, even though the bed is a waterbed (huh?), and the decor and furniture are from 1967, it is clean. Hey, all a road warrior needs is a clean bathroom with a hot shower and a place to plug in the laptop.

Anyhow, I walked for about two and a half hours today and covered about eight miles. I am going to either feel great tonight, or I may pass out. But right now I feel energized.

Broken Bow, in the heart of Custer County, Nebraska, is a wonderful little town. The surrounding farmlands are rich with beef cattle and corn, which is just starting to take hold. And the people who live here are friendly and outgoing.

I would love to see the machinery that rolls the hay here. The bales are twice the size of those at home in Tennessee. There is a big John Deere dealership about a mile away that sells the real stuff! You know, the Big Farm Boy stuff like combines and giant 9000 series tractors.

There is even a McDonalds, a Pizza Hut, a Radio Shack, and a Subway. One really has to love the old Ben Franklin 5-and-10-cent store right off of Broadway. (Broadway??)

But what I really love is the old town square and train station. In the middle of the little park, which is complete with a gazebo (who invented the gazebo, anyway?), there stands a memorial to those young men from Broken Bow who gave all for our freedom. Too many names as usual. I spent some time there.

You see, it's towns like Broken Bow, Nebraska, that are truly the backbone and heart of America. It is not the end of the world.

Maybe they'll build a Holiday Inn someday, but I kind of doubt it. Let's go sing!

OPINIONS

No matter the issue of the moment, everyone has an opinion and the Internet certainly provides a plethora of forums to broadcast it. Anyone can sit in the comfort of their home, log on, and weigh in on politics, current events, religion, pets, lifestyles, war, taxes, terrorism, or even—God help us all—Joe Millionaire.

No matter where your individual interest may reside, there is a chat room or a poll or a message board somewhere on the Internet that provides the freedom for you to exercise your First Amendment right to speak up. Yes or no, for or against, right or left, right or . . . wrong. It doesn't really matter. The fun part is to get involved.

For most of our lives there has been no place where we could go to express ourselves. Our family members and friends already know our feelings, and strangers for the most part just don't care. Those pollsters on CNN and Fox never call us. Who is this guy Gallup anyway? Where is Nielsen or even Zogby? All we get are telemarketers who call us during dinner.

Of course, just about every restaurant, hotel, and Jiffy Lube provides survey forms we can fill out. Rate our friendly service, tell us what you think, blah blah blah. No fun at all. Who ever fills out one of those things?

It would be more fun to call one of those How's My Driving 800 numbers. Does anyone ever do that? I guess if we saw an Orkin truck driving 100 miles an hour through a school zone, we might whip out the iPhone and call that number (after we have called 9-1-1, of course).

However, even that is taking a chance. Just like ordering from Sears. This conversation could (will) be taped. Even if we really despise putting that much on the line for a new set of pillow shams, we do it.

The point is everyone has something to say about most everything, but most folks never got to step up to the plate until now! The Internet has changed us all. Welcome to cyberspace, where you can log on and speak out, either as yourself or by wearing Harry Potter's cloak of invisibility. The lonely, the quiet, the shy can type in CAPS on the Internet. The boisterous, the loudmouthed, the opinionated can be even more, well . . . boisterous, loudmouthed, and opinionated.

Joe and Jennifer   *Photo by Jarrett Gaza*

ON THE TRAIL

October 2, 2004

There is not one thing in this world that beats the big time excitement of taking an active part in a presidential campaign. And on this beautiful day the Oak Ridge Boys find ourselves once again on the trail with our president, George W. Bush, as he seeks re-election.

Actually this is our fifth campaign, which is really quite mind-boggling. It all began in 1988, when our friendship with George Herbert Walker Bush resulted in an invitation to sing at the GOP convention in New Orleans on the very night he was nominated as the Republican candidate for the presidency of our United States.

He had been vice president under Ronald Reagan for the past eight years, and he was pumped and ready for his turn to lead. His acceptance speech was positive and uplifting.

On this magical night when the balloons and confetti filled the Superdome and the whole nation was watching, Bush and his young running mate, Senator Dan Quayle, along with their families, were enjoying their moment in history—and there we were, the four Oak Ridge Boys and our wives, all waving and smiling and singing "God Bless America" right up there on the center stage of American history.

The man who would go on to beat Michael Dukakis and become our nation's forty-first president was singing bass in our ears! And his eldest son was also there sharing the moment with us. How could we have known that we were singing for two future presidents on that magical night in New Orleans?

Now, we didn't do much campaigning in 1988. Just enough to get our feet wet. We learned this much: Our music and our persona could be of help to this great man, and we were honored to put our hearts on the line for what we believe in.

As I have written many times before, knowing George and Barbara Bush has made us better Americans and better people. They have taught us what service to America is all about. Their conservative ideology and their love of freedom and passion for liberty have inspired and strengthened our own feelings of patriotism. They teach by example. Work hard, be honest, honor God, be willing to sacrifice, put your family first, and love your children. This is the stuff that is the backbone of America.

In 1992 President Bush had a real battle on his hands. Even after the successful liberation of Kuwait from the grip of the Iraqi tyrant, Saddam Hussein, in the first Gulf War, and even after a record approval rating of ninety-one percent, President Bush lost the election to an upstart Southern governor by the name of Bill Clinton.

I am proud to say that we stood beside the man right up until election eve. What a thrill for the Oak Ridge Boys! Day after day of motorcades, bus trips, and rides on Air Force One. The plane would land at some airport events, and we would be the first ones off. We would run down the steps, across the tarmac and right up on the stage yelling, *"Four more years, four more years!!"*

Then, while the president would meet and greet all the local dignitaries of that city, we would sing a few songs. After his stump speech, it was back on the plane and off to somewhere else. By the way, young George W. Bush was on those trips as well.

On the eve of the election our last campaign stop was in Louisville, Kentucky. Before we left Air Force One for the last time, we gathered in the office of the president in the front of the plane. In our hearts we all knew that Bush could lose this election. The famous Clinton war room, coupled with a declining economy and a third-party candidate named Ross Perot, were stacking the deck against Bush. And it seemed to all that the end was in sight. At the request of the president the Oaks sang "Amazing Grace." Everyone on the plane wept. Staffers, Secret Service, family, and even a few members of the press corp. It was a moment that has been chronicled in at least three bestselling books.

After the rally we boarded our bus for Hendersonville, Tennessee. It was waiting for us on the tarmac. The presidential limo stopped by the bus, and the voice of George Bush came out of a loudspeaker (no kidding): "Thanks, fellows . . . God bless!"

As our tour bus slid onto Interstate 65 and headed south toward home, we all looked out the window and watched Air Force One take off. For a while it seemed to fly right next to us before gaining altitude and veering off into the southwestern sky toward Houston. The sun was just beginning to set. It was all so beautiful!

We lost the election, but the memory of the campaign of 1992 is burned into the very fiber of our souls—never to be forgotten! Well aware of our willingness to hit the trail for the cause of America, Senator Bob Dole called on the Boys to help him campaign for president in 1996 against the incumbent, Bill Clinton. Here we would go again, searching our tour schedule for a hole or two where we could hit the trail to help a conservative Republican go for the White House.

History tells us, of course, that Clinton won his re-election bid, but once again the Oak Ridge Boys were there. Once again we experienced history, and once again we were honored to crisscross America with a good man who was a blessing to our hearts.

There were also some really funny moments on this campaign. On a two-day tour across Ohio, we rode on the tour bus with Dole. Our job was much the same in about six cities. Jump off the bus, sing a few songs, and fire up the crowd.

On our way to Dayton the senator went to the back of the bus to do an interview with Ted Koppel for that evening's *Nightline* on ABC. The camera crew, Koppel, and Dole were deep into their work as the motorcade neared the town where the next event would take place.

The Dole-Kemp '96 bus had a huge speaker on top, and usually as we entered the rally grounds, Senator Dole would speak to the people from the front of the bus. Well, the streets were lined with supporters and Dole was in the back. So I grabbed the microphone, slunk down, and began to talk like the candidate.

"This is Bob Dole . . . Bob Dole!! Thanks for coming. God bless America! Bob Dole loves Ohio," on and on! On a street corner there was a rather large woman in a polka-dotted dress holding a Clinton-Gore sign. I said, "Welcome anyway . . . nice dress!"

Everyone in the front of the bus was on the floor, including Secret Service and my three partners. It is one of the funniest things I have ever done. I wondered if the senator could hear me from back there.

Well, after the day's events, I found myself in a hotel room watching *Nightline*. There was Dole talking with Koppel in the back lounge of a moving bus. In the background, very faintly, one could hear your author, "Dole . . . Bob Dole . . . "

It was hilarious!

Dole decided to campaign right up to the last minute in an unprecedented ninety-six straight hours on the trail. It was a whirlwind tour that stretched from coast to coast. The Oak Ridge Boys were there for forty-eight hours of it. No sleep at all! Event after event. Starting in California and ending in Knoxville, Tennessee, for us. It was simply amazing. The crowds were great too. Even at 4 a.m. in Phoenix.

Despite our weariness, we sang pretty well. On each stop we would sing two songs, and then listen to Senator Dole and his running mate, Jack Kemp. I dare say that we knew every word of every stump speech by heart!

Senator Dole would lose the election to Clinton, but we learned a lot from this great American. His dedication, his humor, his love of country as well as his amazing energy level, were a true inspiration.

During WWII, in Italy near Anzio, a young Bob Dole was hit so hard in the back with an enemy fifty-caliber bullet that you could see right through him. He paid a heck of a price. He is still crippled today, but the man has never let it hold him back from a life of service to America. I dare say that we have never had a Senate leader as powerful, and we never will. His wife, Elizabeth, is also a marvelous woman, who now holds a U.S. Senate seat in North Carolina. Even his opponent, President Clinton, had nothing but love and respect for the Doles, and so do we!

Yes, we were part of the crazy election of 2000, as well. We rode with George W. Bush on quite a few occasions. There were times when we would fly ahead in a private jet and sing for thirty minutes at a rally in, say, Duluth, Minnesota, and as the Bush Cheney jet would be landing, we would be taking off for a rally in, say, Madison, Wisconsin.

On trips like these we never even saw then-governor Bush! There were other times, however, when we would all be in one place for an event in the usual manner. We even took our own bus tour across the Midwest for several days with a few operatives and performed and spoke at the events with local senators and such on behalf of George W. Bush.

It was a bizarre and very polarized election in 2000, but our guy came out on top, and again we were honored to have made a small contribution to the campaign. There were a lot of dirty tricks played in that election, and we were with George and Laura on more than one occasion when the attacks and barbs from the other side really hurt.

These are fine people. They are patriots. Along with Vice President Dick Cheney and his wonderful wife, Lynn, they have all had a profound effect on our lives.

So here we are in early October 2004, once again riding with the president—our fifth presidential campaign. As in 2000, we have been there for him just about every time the campaign has called us. So far there has not been a tour as such, just an isolated rally here and there that we could fit into our own tour schedule.

Today in Manchester, New Hampshire, about 9,000 supporters have gathered on a pivotal day after the first debate with Democratic candidate Senator John Kerry. The Oak Ridge Boys performed for about thirty minutes before the motorcade carrying President Bush and Senator John McCain arrived.

In a unique and emotional moment the president's mother, Barbara Bush, was waiting to surprise him—and it was all because of us. We had sent her an e-mail telling her about our being in Manchester, and she decided to come and show a mother's support for her son on the day after the nationally televised debate. Once again the Oaks were there for a rather emotional moment in history.

The election is a month away, and I am sure we will be on the trail several more times with the president. This is a meaningful election in which the people of America will decide who is best to lead our nation forward during troubled times when our enemies seek to destroy us because of our liberties, our freedoms, and our regard for life. These evil and barbaric men of terror have no understanding of any of that, so they seek to destroy it. We need a leader who will take them head on in this fight for what is right. It is a noble cause.

The Oak Ridge Boys know that when you take a stand for what you believe in, many will turn on you. Well, let the chips fall. Sometimes putting your heart on the line and standing up for what you believe in is more important than anything. And to a man, William Lee Golden, Duane Allen, Richard Sterban, and Joe Bonsall believe that George W. Bush is the man for this hour in our nation's history.

I guess we will see how it all turns out in November. I know this much. We love our country, and we pray that God will continue to bless us and protect us no matter who is the next president. No matter what side of the fence you are on, we encourage you to vote. That is what our soldiers have fought and died for all these years. Your freedom to vote. Your choice. Keep in mind that many in the world do not have that right!

The Oak Ridge Boys have had a wonderful career so far, and we are very thankful. Our music has provided many opportunities for the Boys to collide with history. We have, in fact, performed in concert for six U.S. presidents—Gerald Ford, Jimmy Carter, Ronald Reagan, and Bill Clinton as well as George Bush number 41 and number 43. We have even been honored on the floor of the U.S. Congress. We have many friends on both sides of the aisle, and we have been privileged over and over again to be in the presence of the men and women who lead our nation. We pray for them all every day.

Keep in mind that, although we have been very much involved in politics all these years and we are four men who study the process closely, we never take our political views to the stage. Although our allegiances are well documented and often very well publicized, we do not feel that people spend their hard-earned money and give of their valuable time to come to a concert and hear a debate on foreign policy or partisan views and ideas. They come to hear the Oak Ridge Boys sing our songs, and that is what we do.

I am also quite certain that none of us will ever run for office. It could be cool, though. President Duane Allen, Secretary of State William Lee Golden, Secretary of the Treasury Richard Sterban, and Secretary of . . . hmm . . . Defense? Not sure. Maybe Joseph S. Bonsall can just write about it all. There would be some hilarious Cabinet meetings, for certain, and we could really have a lot of fun on Air Force One.

Seriously, though, it is not that we are just political junkies or policy wonks. As I said earlier, we really care about America. We love this country with every fiber of our being, and every time we have had an opportunity to serve in some capacity, we have tried to answer the call. Whether it be singing for our troops or for their commander in chief, we are honored and always willing to saddle up and go.

As I come to the end of this little memoir, I find myself wondering if this will be our last presidential campaign. What will we be doing four years from now? If the good Lord is willing and our bodies stay healthy, I would imagine that we will still be out there on tour singing our songs and, therefore, still able to contribute something positive to the process.

Who will run in 2008? There are many possibilities. One has to wonder if the governor of Florida might take a shot next time around. Jeb Bush in 2008? A sixth presidential campaign for the Boys? Perhaps.

See you on the trail!

Addendum

We were indeed back on the trail with President George W. Bush on November 1, the day before the election. After the massive rally in Milwaukee, Wisconsin, that also featured our friends, Brooks and Dunn, we once again stood in a small semicircle backstage with the president and chatted with him before he got into his limo and headed back to Air Force One.

He would then proceed on to Iowa, New Mexico, and Dallas, Texas, while we bussed on back home. With misty eyes the president told us that he believed this was a different day than that last day on Air Force One with his father in 1992. He thanked us for singing "Amazing Grace" that day and told us how much our friendship has meant to his dad as well as to him over all these years.

Surrounded by Secret Service and fully armed SWAT guys, he told us that he would win—and he did! We are thankful for the opportunity to have, once again, ridden with the president of the United States, and we are so thankful to America for re-electing this great man to lead us into the future.

In another commentary, I mentioned that the revival of personal faith in people's lives would be the difference in this election. Following is a quote from that piece.

"I can tell you that since September 11, 2001, the majority of people in this nation are seeking God in their own way. And that is why George W. Bush, a leader who is not afraid to admit that he is a humble man of faith, will win this election!"

I thank God that it proved to be true. If we continue to lean upon and trust in Jesus Christ as a nation, He will hear us. And He will heal and guide our great country.

The liberal idea of taking God out of our lives did not work. It only energized Middle America to vote their hearts, and their hearts spoke Bush! So the campaign trail has ended.

January 10, 2010

Our streak of taking part in presidential campaigns ended with the election of 2008. We were invited by Senator John McCain and Governor Sarah Palin to join them on the trail on several occasions, but our schedule was never able to accommodate their requests. We have known the Maverick, John McCain, for a long time and touring with him would have been a blast. And I would have loved to meet Sarah Palin.

Our new president is Barrack Obama and, although I do not share his vision and left-leaning ideology toward a more socialistic approach to government, I do pray for him every single day. I pray for America every single day!

I am not happy with the overall leadership in the House and Senate, and once again, as I wrote before, I am feeling the winds of unrest blowing hard across America. The politically correct, progressive forces now in power present a clear danger to America, and I think the tea parties and town hall meetings of late reflect the uncomfortable feeling that people are sharing across the Heartland.

It is time for more conservative and God-fearing voices to be heard. It is time for common sense on every level. President Obama campaigned on a promise of change and transparency, but there has been no evidence of that transparency, and the change he has advocated has been to take over health care and big business, grow the national debt, and raise our taxes.

It is my humble opinion that real change will begin in the midterm elections of 2010, and when 2012 rolls around the Oak Ridge Boys just may find ourselves back on the trail.

Who will be running? Who will stand up for all that is right about America? Who will protect us from terrorists? Who will have the courage to keep faith and God in our conversations? Who will stand upon the visions of our Forefathers? Who will stand up to the evildoers and bullies and rogues of the world?

We have never had a perfect president, and we never will. But I believe that God does have a plan and that somewhere out there the right man or woman for the job exists.

So while we wait and see and pray, let's *sing!*

Photo by Darrick Kinslow

As I prepared for Memorial Day 2003, I happened to be digging through some archives at oakridgeboys.com and came across this little "Remember" piece that I did a few years earlier on this very same day. Our webmaster, Jon Mir, does a terrific job of preserving little bits of our memoirs, events, diaries, and history in a past-features section. It is always fun to look back over your shoulder a bit and stare down the pathway from which you just came. It is always thought-provoking to remember!

REMEMBER!

A s I have done many times in the past while in San Antonio, I visited the Alamo.

One is always amazed at the very small size of this old mission fortress. It is literally dwarfed by the big city buildings around it. However, it is the place of Crockett and Bowie and Travis, a place where several hundred Texas Freedom Fighters, with some proud Tennessean Volunteers at their side, gave their lives.

Holding off thousands of Santa Ana's troops day after day, they allowed Sam Houston's Army the needed time to gather and advance. Eventually, while issuing forth the battle cry *"Remember the Alamo!"* they defeated the Mexican Army and liberated the great state of Texas.

One can picture this Alamo sitting alone on the plains with five thousand Mexican campfires lighting up the night. Young, brave, hardened men of battle gathered in prayer. Despite the fear inside, they knew their cause was just.

The same scenario has played out for centuries in war after war, and for the most part liberty and justice has prevailed.

There is a price for the freedom we enjoy in America. Many have paid that price over the years and many are paying it today, for we

153

are still at war against yet another enemy who would threaten to take away our right to live as we do.

So have a great Memorial Day weekend, everyone. Be safe, have fun, and boogie on down. However, make sure that at some point you find a quiet place, bow your head and heart—and remember!

God bless America!

THE RELEVANCE OF "G.I. JOE AND LILLIE" IN 2003

"**M**y son is in Kuwait. . . . "
"I have a neighbor in the Air Force who is right now flying over . . . "
"My cousin has been in Afghanistan for . . . "
"Billy could be shipped overseas any day now. . . . "
"He is a Marine stationed in . . . "
"The 101st just shipped out of Fort Campbell, Kentucky, this morning . . . "
"My brother's unit just got called up. . . . "
"My husband was killed when a Blackhawk . . . "
On and on and on! Sound familiar?

As I read *G.I. Joe and Lillie* last night and once again studied the time period of WWII, I pondered the sacrifice of our nation's best and it hit me—today isn't much different. Our young people are still giving all for the cause of this nation's freedom and protection.

I have a friend, Charlie Keller, who drives for United Parcel Service. He is a hard-working, positive kind of guy whom I have known for quite a while now. He has been delivering packages to our home for years, and I have always liked him.

His son drives a nuclear submarine. Yes, in the Navy they are referred to as boat drivers. He has a young wife and children, and no one knows where he is. He was supposed to come home for Christmas, however, it didn't happen. He could be gone for another six months, which would make this particular tour of duty a full year.

One year! You see, when you drive a nuclear submarine that carries nuclear missiles, your whereabouts are kept secret. Even from your wife.

"Mommy, where is Daddy?"

"He is under the ocean somewhere, honey."

"Which ocean, Mommy?"

"I don't know."

Just like G.I. Joe's Tough Ombres of the Fighting 90th, our men and woman are at war today, and again the sacrifice that is being made is enormous. We are all affected, some more than others.

The Oaks attended a Tim McGraw show recently. A lady handed me a note.

"My husband is stationed in Bahrain right now. He loves you guys. Wait until I tell him that I saw you. He will be so thrilled."

I ran after her and said, "Thank him for me, will ya?"

She cried! She must have been around twenty-three years old. She would go home and write a letter to a boy in a desert and tell him that she saw the Oaks and Tim McGraw and say, "I wish you could have been there, honey!"

So do I.

Faith, loyalty, patriotism, being willing, sticking it out, putting your life on the line and your heart on the table—sacrifice on so many levels.

That sub could sink. That soldier could be killed. That pilot could be brought down. In this uncertain world, so many are paying the ultimate price once again.

Take a stroll through Arlington National Cemetery. Freedom is not free. It never was. It never will be.

In G.I. Joe and Lillie's time our nation was united, much as we were after the horrors of 9-11. Flags were flying. God was being summoned.

Most folks are the same today, even though, if you watch the news, it would seem that we are not quite as united as we could be. To be certain, this is a very emotionally charged time, and I believe many of us are, understandably, a bit confused and even afraid. So much is happening so fast in the world.

I ask you to please keep this in mind even if you do not believe in America's policies or America's leaders, whether you reside on one side of a political ideology or the other, whether liberal or conservative, whether red or yellow, black, brown, or white, whether rich or poor, just remember: *Our freedom to think and to express our views has been paid for in blood and will be again.*

Let us also remember that deep in our hearts we are all Americans. And I believe that we are blessed by God—fortunate to be living in this land of liberty.

Unite on this. Please support our brave troops. Our soldiers, sailors, pilots, and specialists. Our young men and woman. Pray for them. Love them!

Like G.I. Joe and Lillie, they are the best of us!

May God continue to bless the United States of America.

Photo courtesy of Joe Bonsall

THOUGHTS ON "G.I. JOE AND LILLIE" IN 2009

In 2003 the Oak Ridge Boys recorded a very special album project for the Spring Hill Music Group. *Colors* became one of our most popular projects in the last decade. We recorded the CD to honor America and to pay tribute to those who have defended, and now defend, the freedoms of our great country. I believe we accomplished that goal with songs like "An American Family," "Colors," "American Beauty," "The Home Stretch," and "This Is America."

However, another song on the CD, "G.I. Joe and Lillie," has become a YouTube phenomenon. It's hard to find the words to express how deeply moved and humbled I am by it. I'll start with the history of this song, which is chronicled in the Foreword to my book of the same name, *G.I. Joe and Lillie: Remembering a Life of Love and Loyalty.*

Although I wrote the book after my parents passed away, I wrote the song while they were still alive. The Oak Ridge Boys were performing in Lancaster, Pennsylvania, at the American Music Theater, and we had invited forty veterans from the Southeastern Pennsylvania Veterans Home to join us that evening, including my parents. I wrote the song to honor them, and after we performed it that night there was not a dry eye in the place.

G.I. Joe and Lillie left us in 2001. My dad passed away in January and my mom in October. Over the next few years some amazing things happened. I wrote the book based on Lillie's memoirs. It tells the story of a young couple who met after joining the army in the 1940s. Each had grown up in abusive homes. They were a war hero and a WAC who would marry and live with the demons of war for the rest of their lives. Yet they would survive and raise a family. Like the song says, it is a story of faith and patriotism and plain old American grit—desire and hard work. It is my parents' story. But it is similar to so many others'.

The book has been a huge success on every level, as has the song. As a son, I am blessed that I have been able to honor my parents in word and song. I thank God for this every single day. The response has been overwhelming from the beginning, especially from veterans of WWII, who have identified so much with the story. Like the line in the song says, "an American love story not unlike a lot of others." I believe a big reason for the success of the book and song is the fact that so many veterans lived their lives—during that time period and in the years after the war—much like Joe and Lillie did.

A few years ago the Oak Ridge Boys taped a patriotic-themed television special for our friends at Feed the Children. We performed "G.I. Joe and Lillie" live for the first time since that night in Lancaster when I debuted it for my parents. It was a special evening for me, performing with the Oak Ridge Boys on a big stage with the band and all the production. As the cameras rolled, I became incredibly emotional as I sang about my daddy and mommy. I found myself wishing they could be there, and when I got to the last line, "G.I. Joe and Lillie was my father and my mother," well . . . I just lost it.

That television show has played hundreds of times on a number of major networks and helped raise a ton of money so Reverend Larry Jones could feed hungry kids around the world. About a year ago someone put the video of that performance on YouTube. When I first saw it there, I thought it was pretty cool because over the last year quite a few people had viewed it. But that was just the beginning.

Something incredible happened about a month ago when many military Web sites discovered the video and began to embed "G. I. Joe and Lillie" into their homepages, citing it as an example of patriotism and inspiration. The floodgates opened. With well over on million views right now, it appears that people all over the place are e-mailing the link to friends and co-workers. Many who might have never seen it before are watching the Oaks sing the song. I am not sure how far this is going to go, but I will tell you what the bottom line is for me.

Our young warriors are hearing the song and reading the book because of this YouTube happening, and I am hearing from many of them. From Iraq and Afghanistan to military bases worldwide. If my mom only knew that young soldiers of today are reading her story and hearing her song, it would make her very, very happy. She loved every one of them with all her heart. I pray that somehow our Lord will let her know how she and daddy are still touching so many lives.

G. I. Joe and Lillie . . . my mommy and daddy. I love them so much, and I miss them every day. On YouTube? I could have never anticipated that.

God bless our veterans and the young men and women of our armed forces. Keep them safe. Bring them home to those who love them when the mission is complete!

Note: You can watch the video at http://www.youtube.com/watch?v=8lQk27hPzZs

WAR

According to the *Merriam Webster Dictionary,* the word *war* originated in the fifteenth century. Derived from the Old Scottish languages, it simply translates into worst. A few centuries later an Old High German dialect gives us the word *werra,* which means strife and *werran,* which means to confuse.

The modern definition of the word? War—a state of usually open and declared armed hostile conflict between states or nations; a state of hostility, conflict, or antagonism; a struggle or competition between opposing forces for a particular end.

History is, of course, chock full of wars and conflict. Many of them were unavoidable, but many of them could have been resolved with clear vision, moral leadership, strict negotiations, and/or a healthy dose of common sense!

It is the sheer intent that makes the whole scenario of conflict so unnerving. Violence and brutality literally staggers the mind of most human beings, and war is the most vicious of all because the strife inflicted upon fellow humans is carried out on purpose.

We Americans, for the most part, live our lives in a protective bubble of everyday life and our doses of violence come to us as sanitized events filtered through our friends, the television, or a movie screen. These mediums have desensitized us. "Arnie killed 100 guys in that flick." "Look at that train wreck on the news. Wow!" "A plane crashed in New Guinea?" "Another child missing?" "Kids brought guns to school and did what?" "Pass the salt!"

It's not that we don't care. We do! It's just that we see so much bad stuff all the time that we are getting used to it. The Oklahoma City bombing as well as September 11, 2001, woke us up for a while, but many of us have gone back to sleep on the issue. The fact is, we have not witnessed the horror up close, and that, my friends, is the essence of what war is all about.

Death and violence at close range. Ask the Tough Ombres of G.I. Joe's 90th Infantry Division, the old Marines who fought the Japanese in the Pacific, a Korean war veteran, or a Vietnam vet. As I wrote in *G.I. Joe and Lillie,* they probably will *not* talk to you about it. The sheer agony of remembering is too great.

I would guess that folks who witnessed the horror and shock of 9-11 up close carry with them the same trauma. They will never fall asleep on the subject. Their mind's eye and their heart will not let it happen.

On television Gulf War 1.0 looked like a dose of Nintendo, and Gulf War 2.0 looks even more like a video game. The violence of the whole affair is again somehow masked to our senses. But friends, war has never changed, whether it was Samson killing 1,000 Philistines with the jawbone of an ass (imagine that visual) or an atomic bomb dropped from the Enola Gay on Hiroshima. As my daddy used to say, "War is hell!" Having experienced it himself, he never wanted me to see "that hell" and vowed to fight to his own death to spare me the horror.

I imagine that you are waiting for a point to all of this, and I have one. With our blessed nation again at war, I feel the pain and anxiety of the anti-war crowd, and I agree with them to this end: War is a terrible thing, and no one in his right mind could ever want to actually go to war. We are for the most part a God-fearing and God-loving nation, and none of us want to see our precious young people returning home in a flag-draped coffin. However, we cannot ignore the fact that we *are* at war.

There is still a huge hole in the ground in our nation's greatest city that acts as a burial ground for thousands of Americans who were just going to work on that day. Just living in their personal little bubbles, when—boom!—they were overtaken by suffering, carnage, and death. And the same goes at the Pentagon and in a field in Pennsylvania. If not for the heroes on that plane, we might also have a hole in Washington where the Capitol or the White House still stand.

We can never forget this, my friends. Never! If that isn't declared war, then what is?

So, my dear readers, what is the answer? I happen to believe in peace through strength. A bully will beat on you day after day and take your lunch money until you hit him over the head with a milk bottle and make him bleed. That is a fact of life. Walking to school each day, thinking pleasant thoughts, and helping little old ladies home with their groceries doesn't protect you from the fact that there are bad people in the world who are just itching to harm you and disrupt your way of life.

Asking "Why can't we all get along?" and singing "Kum Ba Yah" just don't cut it in this day and age. I really wish it did.

Our present-day enemies are full of unmitigated evil. Groups of fanatics have hijacked an entire religion and twisted it to meet their own miserable purpose—to destroy and dominate. They hate our American way of life. Period. It's that simple

I hate war as much as anyone, but I love freedom and democracy, and there have always been a high price paid and a huge sacrifice made for the blessings of living in the land of liberty. So today I pray as never before that our leaders will be given the wisdom and courage to lead us.

Please understand. I do not possess a blind faith in our politicians. Quite to the contrary. I remember Vietnam, where every mistake that could have been made was! However, I do have faith in God and freedom, and I have put my chips on that hand. I believe the dealer will eventually show a twenty-one. The good guys will win again!

These are tough times. As Americans, we need to pull together just as we did on that September morning of 2001. We need to hit our knees hard, fly our flag high, and support our young men and woman who are right now in harm's way, ready to give their lives for you and for me!

Yes, war is awful and I hate to see it. As an American, a father, and, yes, a grandfather, I also understand that evil must be fought if freedom is to prevail. Tyrants must be toppled if liberty is to prevail, and God must be honored if America is to prevail.

Let's just break that bottle over the bully's head so we can keep our lunch money and go on to school. I really wish there was a better way, but there is not!

WHEN SOMETHING SLIPS

Then shall two be in the field; the one shall be taken, and the other left. Two women shall be grinding at the mill; one shall be taken, and the other left.

—Matthew 24:40-41 KJV

The young and handsome U.S. Marine waited patiently at the front door of the small white two-story house. He stood in silence and stared at the yet unopened door. He searched his soul and tried desperately to find the courage to knock. He knew the family was at home—and not just because there were cars in the driveway.

He could feel them. The boy's keen sense of awareness had already witnessed to him the fact that the family he came to see was certainly inside this house. He was also well aware that this humble home in the mountains had become a house of pain and sadness and immeasurable loss.

What he didn't know was how these folks would react to his presence on their front porch. He would not learn the answer to this mystery until he willed himself to actually go ahead and knock upon the front door. He gathered his emotions. He straightened his impeccably well-pressed uniform and removed his hat and knocked twice.

A woman opened the door. She stepped back a bit and shuddered at the sight of the young Marine in his dress blues. Her eyes welled with tears as she called out to her husband, "Honey, come here."

A well-built man in a plaid shirt and khaki pants suddenly appeared beside the woman. A lifetime of hard farm labor and factory work normally made this silver-haired man a bit intimidating. However, at this moment in space and time, he seemed small, bent, and sad.

Grief can take a very heavy toll on a man, no matter how strong he might appear to be. The man had, in point of fact, not left this home in two months. His eyes were swollen and his expression appeared to be almost blank. He seemed all beaten up somehow. The Marine understood completely.

They all stared at each other for several seconds before the young Marine began to speak the words he had come here to say.

"Sir. Ma'am. My name is Gunnery Sergeant . . . " His own voice began to shake and his words seemed to come from far off . . . very far off. "I was with your son when he . . . when he . . . There was nothing I could do."

The boy choked on his own tears, and he could not finish. The woman stepped forward and took him in her arms. She held him close. The man stepped forward and hugged them both.

Tears fell like raindrops on the front porch of the little farmhouse as a young Marine and the parents of his now-deceased friend dealt with the pain and loss. Perhaps together they could find a measure of healing. That was why he came to this place. He felt the need to meet the family of his fallen comrade, and perhaps he hoped to find a bit of peace in doing so.

As with all veterans of combat from every war since the beginning of time, this young Marine was trying to deal with that which so many brave young men have had to face before him: Why is he here, walking and talking and breathing, while his buddy is not.

This grieving family would do all in their power to befriend and help this young Marine. That is the kind of people they were. Like so many American families, they would rise up and do what they could to help this brave warrior deal with the kind of pain and torment with which they themselves were also too familiar.

Their precious son has become yet another young warrior to join the long line of those who died in the service of country. Gone too soon from this earth and now wrapped in the gentle arms of the Savior.

It would seem that scenes like this have played out across our nation quite often over the last several years. We have been at war with vicious people who hate us for our very way of life, and the price for being in this war always includes sacrifice on many levels. It is an awesome and very meaningful sacrifice.

It has always been thus.

I recently watched the HBO series *The Pacific* and was so moved by it that I read the written accounts it was based on. I recommend to you *Helmet for My Pillow* by Robert Leckie and *With the Old Guard* by Eugene Sledge. In World War II in both the Pacific as well as the European Theater we lost so many of our nation's finest.

It is tough to take. It is always a hard pill to swallow for any generation.

I have had the honor of spending a lot of time with veterans of late. The Oak Ridge Boys recently played a major role in a celebration called Operation Homecoming in Saddle Brooke, Missouri, where we helped to finally welcome home thousands of Vietnam vets and thank them for their service. It was very humbling, to be certain.

We have also performed for our nation's troops several times over the last few years. And I have personally spoken in front of many veteran groups because of my song and book, *G.I. Joe and Lillie*.

I have met so many men and woman who live with memories of war and the carnage that accompanies armed conflict. The young Marine above, as well as my own mom and dad, who now rest in Arlington, would tell you, "No matter what price that one may have paid in combat and beyond, it was those who did not come back who were the real heroes."

I have never met a veteran who didn't feel this way. No, not one!

Bruce Springsteen once wrote a song called "Brothers Under the Bridge." It's about Vietnam veterans who came home from this brutal and unpopular war, lamenting the death of a fellow soldier. He uses the phrase "something slips," which I have never forgotten. I used the phrase in *G.I. Joe and Lillie* in the following context.

> The emotion swells from down deep in the soldier's soul—not due to his own battle trauma—but because the old veteran remembers all the young friends who never came back.
>
> The buddy who was right beside him, living, breathing, and laughing, and then—like the words of an old Bruce Springsteen song—"something slips!" Suddenly, he is gone.
>
> The veteran is constantly overwhelmed to realize that he has lived out his life, earned a living, and raised a family. Yet, if not for the grace of Almighty God and a healthy dose of good luck, he would

be resting on a green hill buried beneath a white cross like so many others who did not live to see the age of 21. A veteran carries these thoughts with him throughout his life like a piece of luggage that is handcuffed to his heart.

Something has slipped many times in Iraq and in Afghanistan and other hot spots around the globe as young American men and woman have been called to serve their country. It has been that way throughout our history and all too often on a given moment in time and space a promising young life has been taken from us. From the Revolutionary War to Vietnam and from the Pacific to Europe, Korea, and the deserts of Iraq and Afghanistan the price has been paid over and over again in blood and in tears. Prices paid! Sacrifice made!

These heroes have died for me.
Yes, it is that personal.
Sacrifice . . . for me!

I wrote a song by that title a few years ago, making the observation that every sacrifice was made for me personally. I truly believe that the soldier in Vietnam, the Marine in Iraq, and the fireman in Manhattan, who all die in the verses of the song, died for me.

As Christ died on the cross for my sins and to provide a pathway to life everlasting, young men and woman throughout time have sacrificed themselves for my rights to live and work and to enjoy and pursue my goals in a free society.

So I can live
In the Land of Free
Raise my kids
Live my dreams
There's a price
For liberty
Sacrifice . . .
For me

Remember these words the next time "something slips" and a young hero is taken from us. Freedom is not free. It never has been!

On the day I first started to write this piece, an MH-47 Chinook helicopter was shot down in Asadabad, Afghanistan. The Chinook was carrying a Night Stalkers Special Ops unit that had been routing out Taliban insurgents in the mountains. Something slipped, and sixteen more American young men made the supreme sacrifice.

No matter what your political persuasion and no matter how you feel about war, please look kindly upon these young men and women of our United States military. They have always served us proudly with honor and valor and have always done what was asked of them. Please thank them when you see them! Love them! Pray for them and for their families!

They are the best of us!
God Bless America!

FAITH

THE THEORY OF CREATIVITY

The creative process. Something that exists today that was not here yesterday. A song. A book. A rebuilt kitchen countertop, or even a new recipe for scampi.

All of these things started out with just an idea or a thought that eventually turned into a real and very solid entity. A completed project. A final edit. Just because someone had the gumption to take another step. Someone nurtured a special desire to go to a new level of thought and process. Someone earmarked some time to actually follow a dream instead of just sitting around moping and hoping that something good might happen.

You see, creation affects our lives in every way imaginable. When someone begins to program their brain's hard drive into the positive pattern of *I can do that* and slowly begins to delete the negative opposite, then good things enter their life.

I believe that everyone has the ability and capacity to create. Many of us are just not in tune with the process. Either that or we have allowed ourselves to sink too far underwater in the sea of negativity. It is a murky world down there. Dark and lonely and filled with loathing and self-pity.

You think I am way out there patrolling left field on this one? A little extreme, perhaps? Drifting around the ozone layer?

Then listen up. Swim on up to the surface with me, and let's begin a marathon of sheer wonder and life-altering excitement. Let's explore the creative process and see if we can apply some of the theory to our everyday lives.

Let's start at the beginning. *The Beginning.* When God—are you ready?—created the heavens and the earth.

By the way, I do believe in the Bible. And I do believe that God created all of this from scratch because He had the power to do so. After all, He is God.

I find this theory a whole lot easier to swallow than evolution. Besides, as George Carlin says, "If man came from monkeys and apes, why are there still . . . monkeys and apes?"

Sorry, Mr. Darwin, although the Galapagos Islands look really cool on the Discovery Channel, it just doesn't wash! I love those big turtles, though.

For the record, I do not believe in predestation either. That old philosophy undermines the whole creative process and makes us weak.

"Oh, that was meant to happen."

Baloney! With all due respect to some of my very dear Presbyterian friends, predestation is a kind of copout theory that definitely stunts one's growth. Why work hard? Why create? Why do anything?

"God has it all planned this way and we can't do anything about it."

What? Would He really breathe life into our souls, and then proceed to take the very act of impulse and creativity right out of our hands? The light bulb was meant to happen? The Holocaust? The Black Plague? The combustion engine? The microchip? The Mona Lisa? The Fifth Symphony? Baseball? The weed eater?

For crying out loud, I could never buy into that. I'll just leave "whatever will be, will be" to Doris Day.

But speaking of baseball, back to the Big Inning. There is no way possible for our finite minds to ever begin to figure out where God was coming from with all this very early creativity. One has to figure that He had somewhat of a plan in mind because God always seems to have one of those. (Predestation couldn't have been one . . . but I am getting repetitive.)

I think it is entirely possible that God might have been a little bored or tired of the status quo or perhaps He just had an idea and followed it up with some viable action.

"Hmm. This could really be interesting. Let Us create the heavens and the earth. Let's split that jewel up into land and water, and let's sprinkle around all kinds of creatures to live there, including that most complex creature of all—man. Followed by an even more complex creature—woman."

What an idea! What a thought! It sure did give Him something to watch over for the next kazillion years.

Some do not believe in God at all. I find that unimaginable because I believe that all creativity and talent comes to us as gifts from above. It all starts with—are you ready?—the Creator! I believe God deserves the title. I mean, just at look what He did with the proverbial "thin air."

The point is that everything starts with a creative idea, and then a follow up. There exists in every human being a small voice of creativity. Whether or not we are in tune with that voice is the $64,000 question.

Are we listening? Are we paying attention when the faucet turns on? Yes, the faucet! That's what I call it anyway.

When the faucet of creativity turns on inside your heart and head, you must let it flow and respond by action. Have you ever had a great dream, woken up, and thought, "Wow, that would make a great book or movie"? Then by noon you were putting Cheese Whiz on your ham sandwich and forgot all about it.

"What was that dream? Hmm. It was good, though. Hey, we are out of Diet Coke!"

A perfect example of not paying attention to the faucet. I am not saying that all ideas come from dreams. It is just an example of not being in tune.

Case scenario: You woke up and wrote it all down while it was fresh. You sat down later and more ideas came to you. Hey, this would make a great story! The faucet was on and you were there. In the game. You wrote some more. Perhaps it all just ended up as a mere exercise and you put it in a drawer, or perhaps it set you on the road to becoming the next John Grisham.

You know, Grisham and Tom Clancy didn't write until well after their original careers were under way. Sidney Sheldon's first book was published after he turned fifty.

The shower is an incredible place of lost—or found—opportunity. I call it the double faucet theory (joking!). I have come up with many ideas while taking a shower. I think everyone has. Because we let our minds go blank a bit while we are cleaning up—and a door opens a little.

The same is true with a long walk, an hour on the lawn mower, and a good day at the beach. We let our minds wander a bit and it is good to do so. I call it clearing the mind—and it is imperative to do that from time to time.

Old Mister Type A who can't relax for a minute and isn't able to get the office out of his head for a while will never create diddly squat

and is a prime candidate for open heart surgery anyway. The same goes for the man or woman who cannot relax and open his or her mind and heart to anything more than thinking about the next meeting or wondering what happened at the last one.

Clearing the mind. What "Hustle Boy" doesn't realize is that a little relaxation away from the grind actually fills your tank with new energy and creativity. I am not talking about a negotiation over a putting green either. I am talking getting away from the grind.

So many of us are running with the needle on the red part of empty. Perhaps we are even trying to be creative and much of it is working out okay. However, it could be even better.

Yes, clear it all a bit. Let the doors open, let the faucet run—and pay attention. This is not hard, gang. Rocket science and brain surgery only really exist for rocket scientists and neurosurgeons—and I hope even they take a little time for that mind-clearing relaxation I am talking about!

Ahhh, this shower feels good. I am so glad I use Dial . . . hmm. A song lyric or a poem comes to you. Are you listening? *Hey, that was good.* Heavily under the influence of Herbal Essence shampoo, do you dare get out of the shower soaking wet and write it down?

I have done it many times. If you do not, it fades into an abyss, just like the forgotten dream that could now be selling on Amazon.com.

Jump off the tractor and write it down, ya'll!

The Book of James tells us that our lives are like a vapor that passes away quickly. God wants us to live a happy, full, and productive life for the short time that we are living within our individual vapors. And creative energy comes from Him—a song, a verse, a book, or a redesigned living room—all a precious gift from Him.

We must pay attention to that faucet of ideas that can come to us at any time. We must keep our heart and mind open to that still, small voice. Our glass must always be half full. Our eyes must see and our ears must hear. We all have the ability to do great things if we will buy into the philosophy of can and will!

I was just taking a shower at a Hampton Inn in East Lansing, Michigan, when my faucet turned on and the ideas for this little essay came to me. I am still a bit damp as I work at my laptop. These words that I am now writing will end up on my Web site as a commentary, and then maybe age in a desk drawer. Or it could be the start of new book. A book that doesn't exist today. But next year, who knows?

The Theory of Creativity by Joseph S. Bonsall could be on next year's *New York Times* bestseller list. People everywhere could be leaving their long, hot showers to write screenplays while dripping on the carpet.

Hey, it could happen! Then I'll be really glad that I was paying attention when God turned on the faucet!

Clear your mind. Go create something!

SPRINGTIME

"just so many summers, and just so many springs"
—From *The Last Worthless Evening* by Don Henley, John Corey, and Stan Lynch

"Stop and smell the roses."
—Mac Davis

Someone actually told me once that springtime made her sad. When prodded as to the why behind this incredible statement, this person explained that she was much happier in the wintertime. "Give me a dreary, cloudy, and cold day anytime. Spring reminds me of death, and it makes me sad. Yes, things grow, but then they die!"

As my good friend Duane Allen might say, "Well, double duh!"

How can a person's fear of death or anything else prevent one from enjoying this precious time of rebirth and, yes, optimism? That's a bad word for the glass half empty crowd, who would rather wallow around in self pity and defeat while the dogwoods are blooming.

As a baseball fan, I love the fact that my Phillies—and your Cards or Mariners or Diamondbacks—all start the year with a fresh slate. 0 and 0, baby. We are all in first place in April.

Of course, October is another story. When the leaves turn colors, every team but two is all but gone, and just one (probably the Yankees) wins it all.

But, hey, wasn't that fun? Yes, except for maybe the Chicago Cubs fans out there. But didn't even you think that they had a chance this year? Sure you did! Optimism!

Spring makes me feel that way. I will never be able to go the other direction on this. Sure, the daffodils and tulips and bridal wreaths only bloom for a little while, and then they are gone for another year. But while they are here, wow!

The warm air, the new leaves, the bright floral colors all speak volumes. I believe a cardinal or a tulip is red as God meant it to be. The same with the green of a new leaf or the blue of a clear sky. The yellow color of a goldfinch is, yes, yellow!

Sounds obvious, but so many people miss out on these observations and blessings. Ah, yes, did I mention birds? I love birds!

I have been asked many times, "Tell me something about you that your fans and friends might not know. Something that would surprise them."

My answer is usually centered around my farm. Most people cannot picture this old Philadelphia city boy sitting on a big John Deere tractor cutting a big pasture, so that answer is usually sufficient. Only my singing partners and my precious family know of my real passion for birds. I have loved them since I was a kid, and even that is kind of strange, I guess. The only birds that seemed to live on Jasper Street were English sparrows and dirty old pigeons. But come spring, Mr. Robin Red Breast even came to Philly, and I always loved him.

I had these little plastic bird models on my dresser right next to my model planes and tanks and jeeps. I put them together myself. Not always a good thing. I am not very artistic. My mother spent a lot of time scraping drops of Ducco cement off, well, a lot of stuff. My little bird models weren't very well put together, but I loved them.

Even today on my shelf at home I have about twenty little wooden collectibles of birds of all kinds. Mary buys them for me from time to time, and they are very well put together. No caked up glue or paint bubbles anywhere.

If you cannot sit down for a while and enjoy the sweet song of a meadowlark or the coo of a mourning dove or the kee kee sounds of a killdeer, then I feel kind of sad for you. If the flight of a red-tailed hawk or the nest-building prowess of a barn swallow doesn't move you in some way, maybe you need to slow down a little and take notice. Hey, I am performing over 200 shows this year, plus promoting a book, and I find the time. In fact, I believe it is imperative to do so.

A mild spring day. Mary and I, building a flower garden. Mulch and dirt in my fingernails. The smell of freshly cut grass and honeysuckle floats by on a dream. The distant sound of a woodpecker hammering on an oak tree. The turkeys and deer preparing to mate so that we might have more turkeys and deer.

Early evening as dusk builds into darkness, the bullfrogs begin to croak out their droning and amusing mating call as the ponds and creeks begin to come alive. The crickets and tree frogs chirp while a million or so lightning bugs blink across the pasture like some obscure Disneyland.

This is life, folks, and this is living! Only so many springs.

Sure death is around the corner, but isn't it always? Besides, Jesus took care of that little concern on the cross of Calvary. In Him we have eternal life and life more abundantly while we dwell on this planet.

My Bible tells me that man is appointed once to die, but if our hearts are right with God, there is no sting in death and no victory whatsoever in the grave. So why concern yourself with that? It is simply a waste of good time and energy that could be spent enjoying the aforementioned abundance, which is manifested so beautifully in springtime.

In the classic gospel song, "Come Spring" written by Dottie Rambo, her mother rejoices in the fact that before the roses grow in her garden, she will be with Jesus. She hates to miss the coming magic of the season, and she probably never realized that the last spring would be her last. But she is okay with this because as a born again Christian she knows that her next season will be spent with the One who gave us springtime to begin with. Imagine springtime in heaven! Whoa now!

My good friends, while we are still breathing oxygen into our present-day bodies, I beseech you. Please take a moment. Sit down on a rock by a creek side for a while and enjoy God's gifts. Clear your mind and open your heart to God and His Son. Let some optimism into your life. These are tough times but not really much different or tougher than any other time.

To the Bobby McFerrin song of a few years ago "Don't Worry, Be Happy" I will add, "Trust in Him with all your heart and soul, and He will bless your life beyond comprehension—in this season and well beyond."

Perhaps He will open your eyes to the amazing beauty of springtime, just in case you are so busy that you are missing out on it.

Take that day in the country. Smell the flowers, watch the birds, listen for the symphony. We only have so many springs.

Celebrate life.

MUSING ON HEAVEN

I have a very dear and special friend by the name of Lo-Dee Hammock. Lo-Dee was raised in Texas and presently resides in either Florida or Branson, Missouri. I have known her for almost twenty years now. I met her when she was a young bus-tour director. She is the most energetic and inspiring woman I have ever known this side of my own mother.

Lo-Dee is now ninety-two years old and, although fighting some illness, she has not slowed down very much. The only indication that she has aged at all is the fact that she now needs to use a walker to get to her car, which she still drives.

This blessed woman is an angel on this planet, and over the years and perhaps especially more of late, I find myself in her presence discussing heavenly as well as earthly things. I love her dearly, and when the Good Lord decides to take her home to Glory it will sure leave a big hole in my heart as well as in the hearts of all the people she has touched and blessed.

The Oak Ridge Boys play in Branson more than any other town. Of our 150 plus days on the road each year, we work about thirty in Branson. Many of these engagements come in three-day increments, and just about every one of those days I visit with Ms. Lo-Dee.

We laugh, we catch up with each other, we share blessings, and we pray and sometimes even cry together. Like Mitch Albom's *Tuesdays with Morrie*, my visits with Lo-Dee have become a fabric of my being. She is indeed my second mother.

On this day, Thursday, October 15, 2009, we shared an incredible few hours talking about what we know and do not know about death and heaven. One might assume that a ninety-two-year-old may be closer to the end of the journey than a sixty-one-year-old singer, writer, and half-baked banjo player. However, one of the things we do know for certain is that the grim reaper has no respect for age. A walk through any graveyard and a hard look at the markers will prove that point very quickly.

Another thing we know is that "It is appointed unto man and every other living creature once to die," so we are all going. What most of us don't know is the time or the place or how it all might end.

I also know from experience that, although Jesus has prepared a wondrous place for us, nobody has a burning desire to hasten the trip. The ability to breathe air and live on this earth is one of God's greatest gifts. I have seen friends, loved ones, and even animals, fight with everything inside them to stay alive. Death is not very pretty, but the journey beyond is full of mystery and wonderment.

Just what is really over there? What is heaven really going to be like? Unlike the unbeliever, I do believe in heaven. I cannot imagine that when a soul leaves that empty shell of a body behind it wanders off into some eternal darkness or, worse yet, comes back as a frog. Quite frankly, with a little bit of faith and knowledge of the Bible, the hereafter that Jesus speaks about is a lot easier to believe. So on this day Lo-Dee and I muse on about heaven, and I am about to share these random thoughts.

We know that one day we shall pass on. Every living thing at one point or another will eventually go back to being part of the earth. Ashes to ashes. Dust to dust. Death is an end, yet it is a beginning for those of us who believe in Jesus Christ as a personal Savior. But what happens after we cross that old, chilly Jordan is as much a mystery now as it has ever been. Oh, lots of people have written about near-death experiences, where they saw the Light or God or other glorious sights, and perhaps many of these ring true. It is very possible, but it is hard to know with certainty.

Lazarus came forth from the dead at Christ's command, but I do not remember reading very much about his experience. Where did you go, Laz? What was it like? Never addressed. After Christ died on the cross, He seemed quite busy over the next three days. He even went to hell and confronted Satan, proving to all the minions of heaven and below that it was *He* who held the keys of life and of death. He proved it by rising up from the tomb. Christ conquered death and in so doing showed all to come that His promises were true and very much forthcoming.

He said, "I go to prepare a place for you that, where I am, there you will be as well. My Father's house has many mansions." The songs and hymns of the gospel contain a plethora of verses regarding streets of purest gold and walls of jasper and gates of pearl, yet these could all be just metaphors for something so glorious that our human mind could never fathom it.

If mansions or crowns or perhaps a jeweled walkway were what we really desired, I might suggest that would be a bit shallow. Heaven will be much more than that, and I think that real saints of God are looking forward to the other aspects with more anticipation. Although I'll bet that my wife Mary will be looking forward to every jewel she can lay her hands on. Just kidding, honey!

Will we know each other in heaven? You bet! We will be known as we are known! This is my favorite promise. I think when I see those loved ones, who have gone on before, residing in perfect and healthy new spiritual bodies, that perhaps in one glance I will see them at every age.

I will see a young Lillie, while at the same time seeing my mom at a later time, and she will be so very happy. She will know me as well in the same way, and she will hold me for as long as she cares to hold her son because passing time will not be an issue in eternity.

There will be great rejoicing and homecomings and tears of joy and happiness. Yes, this sounds like the heaven that God speaks of when He says that no good thing will be withheld from us.

Perhaps it will be multi-dimensional, where layer after layer of places exist. Maybe just by thinking or wishing for something it will happen. I want to see Jesus . . . there He is. I want to chat with Abraham Lincoln . . . it happens. I want to laugh with my daddy . . . it happens. I want to see my Nana Gertrude Clark or Ms. Lo-Dee. There they are. Just like that!

I like to believe that there will be animals there. Lions will not only lie down with lambs, but precious pets who meant so much to us on earth may appear at the mention of their name or the celestial thought of the memory of them. Where is my kitty Pumpkin? There he is! Where is my little Omi cat? He is right there!

There will be light and flowers and music the likes of which our human form could have never imagined. Angels and saints singing praise to the King! Choirs and instruments galore, and if I think about my singing friends who have gone on, then there they will be. George Younce and Glen Payne, James Blackwood and Sister Vestal Goodman, just to name a few. I may sit down by the river and listen to some great Southern-style gospel music for a long time. Then I will join in the singing.

Jesus will be on every level of this wonderful place. He will shine a perfect light upon all of us who have accepted Him as Lord and Savior and King of our lives, and His constant love will burn and shimmer within our spirits. The feeling will be one of pure joy on a level unimagined on this earth.

So then, those are the musings of Joe Bonsall and Lo-Dee Hammock on a beautiful fall day. What may come to be and what may not come to be are truly not known by any of us. But it is fun to think about, and it is a blessing and a comfort to know that farther along we will know all about it! Farther along all our questions will have answers, as is His promise. I am standing on these promises of Christ, our Lord.

In the meantime we live our lives here and live them more abundantly, thanks to our faith in Jesus. This life below is a wonderful journey, indeed, and I am thankful for every single day. I am thankful for my family and for my friends, and I am thankful for songs that are sung and words that are written.

One day we will sit in Glory and reflect upon these days. We will be healthy and strong, and we will be surrounded by friends and loved ones. This we do know! To quote the great gospel songwriter, Jim Hill, "What a day glorious day . . . that will be!"

There

We are appointed to pass
To a wonderful land
That has been promised
Long ago. . . there
The Lamb, the star
The Savior, the lily
God's only Son
Has prepared the way. . . there

His blood was shed
On a lonely hill
So that we the lowest
Might live forever. . . there
We shall abide with him
In heavenly light
Surrounded by loved ones
In unimaginable glory. . . there

Our finite minds
Can no way fathom
The eternal promise
That awaits us. . . there
Do we fear the river
That we are appointed to cross?
No, for the way the truth
The life will lead us. . . there

What promise
What joy
What singing
What beauty. . . there

DOTTIE AND MILDRED (SPRINGTIME 2)

My comments on the joys and blessings of springtime have brought about a couple little side stories, and I would like to share them with you. First of all, along with the birds and flowers, it was Dottie Rambo who inspired me to share my deep feelings on my love of springtime. Now that April is past and we are steaming on into May, perhaps a time of reflection is in order.

The Oak Ridge Boys taped a new television special at the end of March 2003. The patriotic show called *Let Freedom Sing* was based on the music from our album *Colors.*

The special was broadcast over many cable TV stations throughout the summer of 2003 and beyond. We were honored to have President George Herbert Walker Bush tape the show's introduction as well as having the association of our friends at Feed the Children. We hoped the show would not only be uplifting but would raise money that would be used to help feed hungry children around the world.

Our album co-producer, Michael Sykes, was studying the final sound mix and video of the show when legendary gospel songwriter Dottie Rambo walked into his studio. The song on the screen was "G.I. Joe and Lillie" as performed by your author and the rest of the Boys. As the song permeated the room, she sat next to Michael and began to weep.

"You know, I have never known that boy very well," she said. "I have met him in passing over the years, but I seem to know Duane, William, and Richard so much better than him. This song is wonderful. What a blessing, what tenderness."

She proceeded to shed a few more tears, then prayed for me and left the studio. My good friend and associate, Michael, was so blown away by the moment that he called me immediately and shared this moving event.

I was likewise moved to tears because I have always believed that Dottie Rambo is one of the greatest songwriters of our generation. To think that she was so moved by a song of mine was mind boggling to me. I felt so very humbled.

Dottie was right. She didn't know me that well. I had never had the opportunity to talk much with her over all these years, but I love so many of her songs, and I found myself singing "Come Spring," one of my favorites, for the next several days.

I just couldn't get the song—or Dottie—out of mind. So I called her. What a blessed time we had. She was so sweet. She shared much of her life story with me. She told me about her songs and about her mother's passing, which was the inspiration behind "Come Spring."

I told her of my life and about "G.I. Joe and Lillie," the song and the book. She asked me to pray for her because her health "wasn't that good these days." We laughed and we cried, and then we prayed together.

Now perhaps you can understand the reason I wrote my little springtime piece. I started writing it as soon as I hung up the phone that day. The next day I sent the essay as well as a copy of *G.I. Joe and Lillie* to Ms. Rambo.

Ah, but there is more. When you write a song or a poem or perhaps a book, you put your heart right out there on the table and always hope that there is a reason and a blessing in store for the work. I wrote "Springtime" and put it up on my website. About a week later, I asked my associate, Kathy Harris, to send it to a few local newspapers as sort of an op-ed piece. I didn't think much more about it until I received a call from Mildred.

Mary and I were on the farm, working hard, for about three days. When I wasn't doing book interviews for *G.I. Joe and Lillie,* I spent hours at a time dragging a six-foot Woods finishing mower behind my small Deere 4300 or strapped to a Shindowa weed eater. One thing about spring, the grass and weeds explode like cruise missiles, and here in the holler on the Monroe-Macon county line one had better keep it under control or the whole farm might disappear!

Soon it would be time to tackle the big fields, but not yet. I had just put the tractor in the barn when my wife, "Garden Girl," called me. "You have a message on the machine from Mildred. I sure haven't heard from her in a while."

Neither had I. Mildred was a casual acquaintance whom we had known for years. She shipped packages at a Pony Express store in Hendersonville when we first met her. More recently she was a waitress at the Gamaliel diner and served Mary and me breakfast quite often. Always friendly, always smiling, always talking away about this or the other, the woman was a sheer joy, and we liked her a lot.

One day a few years ago she left the diner. We heard that she was working at the American Greetings plant in Lafayette, but we weren't sure. We had heard a year or so ago that she wasn't doing well, but as you know, time moves on.

"Mildred? Wow, I haven't seen her for years. I better call her," I said.

"Oh Joe, thanks for returning my call. I have had your number for five years, and I finally used it. It is so nice to hear your voice. How are you guys?" she asked with that smile and laugh in her voice.

What a sweetheart, I thought.

"Mary and I and the Boys are all doing great, Mildred. How about you?"

"Joe, I have cancer and I am dying. I have been fighting it for two years now. I have had eleven operations in the past year alone, and the chemo has worn me plumb out. The doctors have told me that I probably won't see my sixty-fifth birthday this June."

I was stunned. What a shame. I moved my lips to Mary. "Cancer . . . poor Mildred."

Mary sat down hard on the couch.

"I am sorry, Mildred. Anything I can do?"

"Oh, Joe, you already have. That is why I am calling," she said, still seeming to be bubbling over with joy. "When my *Tomkinsville News* came yesterday, right there on page two was your article about springtime. It was just what I needed. I was feeling so down, and your words really made me stop and think. I got right down on my knees and thanked God for His blessings and for this wonderful time of the year so filled with His love. After reading it, the flowers became brighter to me and the birds sang so much sweeter. Thank you and God bless you!"

So you see, you never know. Had Dottie Rambo not walked into Michael's studio at that time, she never would have thought of me, and

I would never have called her and spoken with her about her blessed song "Come Spring." Without Dottie, that song would never have crossed my mind, and I might never have written the essay. If Kathy had not sent it to the *Tomkinsville News,* Mildred would never have seen it and called me at the farm.

Until her phone call I didn't even realize that the piece was published in that paper. I had no idea.

Perhaps God meant for "Springtime" by Joseph S. Bonsall, inspired by Dottie Rambo, to be read by Mildred in Gamaliel, Kentucky, that day so she would notice and appreciate His wondrous beauty here upon this earth just one more time before she made her blessed trip to heaven to be with Him.

Any doubts? None here! Celebrate life, and please say a prayer for Dottie and Mildred.

Note: Dottie Rambo was killed in a bus accident in 2008.

BIG FIELDS

Our lives appear to be more fast-paced than ever before. The pace has picked up, and our personal calendars and to-do lists are jammed full. People cannot stop moving and shaking and sharing. Facebook, YouTube, MySpace, Twitter, and a whole host of other such social networking Web sites keep people of all ages busy every day. Your author is as guilty as the next person of using these outlets in a good and productive way, and yet I am also just as guilty of wasting a ton of time online. I can't help it. To paraphrase Neil Diamond: I am, I said . . . I am, I tweet . . . I am!

Most of us live our daily lives just so we can blog about it later on. I guess I am doing that right here and now upon this page. I do enjoy blogging from time to time and, as stated, I like the Twitter thing—creative little blurbs in 140 characters or less. I can deal with this. Every goofy little thought that makes its way across my brain has the potential to become a Tweet. Twitter is actually kind of like being embedded deep inside of an eclectic circle of friends and listening to them think out loud—fun, if not a bit scary at times. But I do enjoy it!

Besides, stuff like this gives people something to do, and most of all it is innocent and fun. Quite frankly, this little commentary is not about how we spend our days or spare time. It is certainly not about the Internet but just a means to get your attention and to provide for you an example of the little things that really do not matter very much in the big picture.

What really matters is how we will get through the Big Fields when they appear before us. What will we do when the burdens add up to unbearable or the task ahead begins to seem impossible to fathom. I know this much is true: When the big storms blow in and upset your applecart, things like Facebook or MySpace are not going to pull you through. The Internet will not help you. You will have to rely totally on your inner-net for this. It will be gut-check time. Do not adjust your set. This is not a test but an actual alert.

Little things will not matter when you come to the Big Field. Handwringing over small stuff generates a negative energy that can render forward thinking and needed strength almost impotent at a time when you will need it most. When your faith is tested it is best that you have faith to begin with because you can be very certain you will need it! There is a wolf waiting in the bushes and when he inevitably comes out of hiding and actually knocks upon your front door, you had better be prepared. The Piper has arrived, and he will want to be paid.

Everything in your life may have been perking along just fine, and then *boom!* You can become a ball seemingly lost in the high weeds of a pasture that seems never ending. To continue through life, you will have to navigate correctly and cut down the weeds that impede your progress, for you surely do not want your journey to end in a place like this. Many have never found their way out of this field.

This Big Field of which I speak is an obvious metaphor for a major health issue or a financial burden or a serious falling out with your loved ones. Perhaps your wounds are all self-inflicted. Alcohol or drug abuse could be the reason you have been dumped here. Depression or self-pity or low self-esteem is responsible for dropping many a good man or woman of every age into these weeds. Perhaps you have lost a loved one, and you feel there is no way out from under the weight of your heavy heart. Perhaps you have just caught a few bad breaks and have found yourself walking beneath the darkest of skies.

No matter what has brought you to this dark place, it is now reckoning time. Time to mount up, draw your sword, and fight! It is time to do battle against whatever it is that is impeding your life, and you are the one who has to do it. Yes, it will be difficult, but sometimes the only one who can get it done for you is you! This is your life, your vapor, and it is passing quickly. There is not really much time.

When waves of darkness and doubt and pain have laid us down, it is hard to get up. But I assure you, my friends, you can and you must get up. You must pray for inner strength, and then use that spirit-driven power. Kick hard and make your way toward the surface and the light lest you drown and fade away in your own despair!

God has created the human being with an incredible will and a fierce fighting spirit. This spirit of survival is much stronger than the will to languish. The right is still stronger than the wrong, and the light is still brighter than the darkness. The healing power of Jesus is still more powerful than any pain this world can press upon you.

You must cling to the positive. Easy? No! Doable? Yes, it is!

Jesus Christ has taken every care, every burden, and every sin from us already with His love and sacrifice. He says to simply lay all our cares and burdens upon Him. We will never be given more than we can handle, and He will be there always with a yoke that is lighter and much easier to handle. With Jesus in our hearts and lives, the Holy Sprit there to minister, and everlasting arms to lean upon, we now have help—and perhaps a roadmap with which to navigate our way forward through this Big Field. But be assured, it is a process.

When a farmer faces a big field that needs sowing or cutting, he doesn't fret about the size of the field or dwell upon how long it will take him to do what needs to be done. He just starts working. After a while there is a dent, and after some perseverance and passing time, the farmer finds that half the field has been plowed or cut.

Perhaps after a rest and some nourishment he climbs back aboard the tractor and continues with the task at hand. There may be a stumbling block or two along his way, a hole he did not see, a flat tire, or something else not planned. But the farmer deals with the setbacks and keeps on going. He is not in a hurry. He is patient in his approach. He will not be deterred.

At last he is finished. The field has been worked. It looks good, and now the farmer can go on home, put his equipment in the barn, and have dinner with his family. The heavy task that was before him at dawn has now passed on before him, and all is well. The Big Field has been overcome due to the hard work of the farmer.

So just start plowing, friends. With God's help the big, weedy field will one day become clear and green before you. You will have won the battle, and you can now move onward and upward in your journey. In the great scheme, the weeds do grow back. But each time you persevere, you gain a bit more insight, experience, and knowledge, and you become more aware of the dangers and the setbacks. Therefore, each cut becomes a bit easier.

Faith, perseverance, and love all play a part in this resurrection of spirit, but remember that patience is a big key. You didn't suddenly fall. You will not suddenly get up either, so pray for patience. It is so important to take one day at a time, one step at a time, one pass at a time.

Soon the Big Field is cut, and you can come back home to where you belong, living in the light of the love of Jesus Christ with the weeds of darkness all cut down! It is called victory! It is called living the way God wants you to live. Not groveling around in despair, but rather walking tall with new purpose upon a freshly cut field. With Him by your side.

BRE AND LUKE

I glance around Chuck E. Cheese's and notice that my fifty-five years makes me the oldest person in the place. Along with about sixty or seventy children running back and forth between video games and such, I see mostly young mommies or daddies in their twenties or early thirties.

All these young parents seem to possess that same tired look that I see in the eyes of my oldest daughter. Raising kids is not for the lazy or the squeamish. You cannot begin to match their energy level, but you have to always figure out a way to keep up with them.

I take a bite of pizza. Hmm, not a bad pie.

"Pop Pop, come here and look," yells a handsome little four-year-old boy who has just mastered a game wherein some animals pop up out of holes and he hits them on the head with a hammer. It takes just one token, and as Pop Pop has provided him with a whole cup of tokens, these poor creatures are really in for some trouble.

BONK...... "Owwwwwww, hahaha!" Nothing like the laughter of a grandson.

"Cool, Luke, you are really good at that one. Look at all the tickets you are winning," I exclaim as I watch a beaver take a hit. BAM!

You see, each game awards the children tickets that can be redeemed on the way out for all kinds of little toys and gifts, which brings me to Breanne. At age eight, she is simply beautiful. The walking image of her mother Sabrina and her Mom Mom, my Mary. It's amazing to see the woman I love so represented in the life force of my granddaughter.

Bre is playing skee-ball. Good old skee-ball, a game that hasn't changed in a hundred years. Roll the ball down the little alleyway and up it flies, eventually landing in one of several holes, each one progressively harder to hit. The more difficult holes award more cumulative points, and Bre is racking up tickets.

"I am really, really good, huh, Pop Pop?" Bre smiles. (Hello, Mary. Hello, Sabrina.)

"You are the best, hon. Are you guys finished eating?" I yell loud enough for Luke to hear.

"I am full, Pop Pop." BONK. "Ooww," Luke yells with glee.

"Yes! Yes! Yes!" says Breanne. "One more game though, okay?"

Okay! I start to gather up all their tickets, and we eventually make our way to the little redemption center at the front of Chuck E. Cheese's. A very cool place really. Good food, lots of games, children running around and laughing. A little carnival by the mall. As John Mellencamp might say, "Ain't that America?"

Between the three of us (I did shoot some hoops and earned a few myself), we had about 280 tickets. Plenty for a space gun for Luke, but well short of what was required for a Barbie makeup kit. I grabbed Breanne before she headed back for the skee-ball game and proceeded to negotiate with the eighteen-year-old behind the counter who had a pin sticking through her nose. Miss Pierce eventually sold me the Barbie kit and everyone was happy.

Especially me. You see, I am a man of the road, and over all of these years I have missed a lot of good home stuff. I am not complaining for God has blessed me with a great career, and I have always believed that for everything worthwhile there is a price to be paid. My sacrifice has been missing a lot of quality time with my daughters, Jennifer and Sabrina. Now I am a grandfather taking two beautiful children to Chuck E. Cheese's, and then to a movie about a talking mouse. Pop Pop is on cloud nine. We sing and tell jokes as we drive around town.

"You know why there is a fence around the cemetery?" I ask.

Bre and Luke scream the answer together as one, "Because people are dying to get in there!"

"You know how many people are dead in there?"

"All of them!"

More laughter and carrying on.

"Shut your little pieholes!" I yell and that brings on more laughter.

I finally pull into the driveway of their home where Mommy and Daddy are waiting to put the two very sleepy kids to bed. I drive off amazed at how many sour gummy worms a four-year-old boy can eat during one movie, especially after pizza at Chuck E. Cheese's.

The cell phone rings. It is Mom Mom. "How did it go?"

"Just great, hon, just great! I'll be home soon."

Often Mary and I take the grandkids out together, but tonight it had been decided that just Pop Pop should take them, and, as always, I never forget my time with these children. Each memory is as clear as crystal.

You haven't lived until you ride around in big circles on a John Deere tractor with a little grandchild fast asleep on your lap. Taking them fishing or to a movie or playing catch or a game of Checkers or Trouble can be as refreshing as a summer rain. Being a grandparent allows you to spoil them rotten, and then . . . take them home. That is all part of the Great Plan, I guess, and it certainly works for Mary and me. You should see Christmas!

After arriving back home I cannot help reflecting upon the circle of time that is passing before me. Two empty bedrooms now exist where once slept the two beautiful little girls who grew up under our own watch.

My Jennifer, who is now twenty-nine, and my Sabrina, who is thirty three, have each turned into wonderful and responsible young women who, thankfully, each married a strong, sturdy, and hard working all-American boy. And for all of this I am very thankful.

Jen lives in Florida and is now a vice president of a cutting-edge marketing firm, and Sabrina who lives right here in Tennessee is an interior designer, as well as being mommy to Bre and Luke.

The responsibility of bringing up Bre and Luke does not rest with Mary and me. We are on the periphery, as we should be, lending support and help when needed and, quite frankly, enjoying all the good parts.

However, the same old worries still exist. Will they be healthy? Will they be sane? Will they survive driving and college and fads and friends? Will they make something positive out of their opportunity to live in America, or will they be a constant heartbreak to their parents?

As a father, I have been through this process already and, let's face it, there is just so much we can do. The rest is always a crapshoot and, hopefully, God in His infinite wisdom is guiding the roll of the dice.

As a Pop Pop, I constantly ask God to protect these little ones who are now a part my life. One day a few years back I received some very positive direction, and it came from my granddaughter.

When Breanne was a few months shy of turning three years old, we had a conversation that I will never forget as long as I live, a conversation that brings me comfort to this very day. We were sitting on the floor of her bedroom, and she was describing for me in a very serious fashion the different creatures who lived under her bed and in her closet. I was fascinated.

"Daddy says that it is just my 'imaginationum,' but I can see them all quite clearly, Pop Pop," she said.

"Well, spirits and beings do exist, Bre. The Bible even says that they do," I answered.

"They are real, Pop Pop, and I can see them!" she insisted.

She proceeded to explain their colors and shapes and demeanors, and I found myself totally absorbed. I had never had a conversation like this in my entire life, and I felt honored that she was sharing her heart with me.

A few quiet moments passed.

"Are any of these guys bad?" I asked.

"Some are."

"Do you get scared of them?"

"Nope! You see, Pop Pop, nothing can hurt me because of the angel. He protects me. He is from God." She was smiling now and looking so beautiful.

"Is he in the room now?" I asked as my spine tingled just a bit.

She whispered as if sharing a secret, "I can't always see him, Pop Pop, but he told me that he is always here for me, and I believe him."

Then so do I.

May God always keep a watchful eye on Bre and Luke.

SOMEDAY WE WILL KNOW

I just read a piece by a very inspiring writer and friend, Tiffany Truitt. You can find her writings at tiffanytruitt.blogspot.com.

In her short but moving blog she writes about the heartbreak of a little girl in line for a transplant while some other person she knows killed himself.

I identified with this just recently as we buried our good friend Todd Brewer, who lost a battle with cancer at forty-two years old. He fought with all his heart and soul. He so wanted to stay with his beloved wife and children, but God saw it differently, for there he lay before us in his coffin in his favorite overalls while the U.S. Navy folded his flag.

As I sat in that pew in the Hendersonville Memorial Gardens, it hit me that just a month or so ago I sat in this same place saying goodbye to a friend named Stacy Briggs. Stacy was also forty-two years old and was in perfect health on the afternoon that he decided to wrap an electric cord around his neck and jump off his back deck.

So easy to ask why, so easy to ponder a different course for both young men. As Christians we must take comfort in the fact that God is in control of our lives, but as humans . . . well, to be honest, it can be quite bewildering. A viable test of our faith, to be certain.

I have no astounding ending to this little piece. I just want to provoke you into being thankful for that which God gives to us everyday: the precious gift of life! Celebrate and honor it! In the big picture and in the grand scheme of things we are not really here that long anyway, so while you are celebrating be sure to lay aside some quality time for preparation for the journey that lies ahead of all of us.

One way or the other we will all take that mysterious trip when the very temporary body we live in at the moment gives way to death, and then victory when we will live in the light of the Lord and all things will be made clear to us. Why one is taken and one is not. Why a little girl has to wait for a heart and even why a friend ends his own life. We will understand it all better in the By and By. Make sure you are there!

God bless, friends.

A WINTRY DAY

During the busy touring season when the bus is rolling down the highways day after day after day, and the shows and the songs and the hotel rooms are flying by like so many flecks on the Rand McNally, one has a lot of time to think about what one might be doing when that precious home and vacation time is here at last.

It had been a busy 2009 overall, and the Christmas tour was as long and aggressive as a tour could be. So everyone was ready to get home and attempt to be normal for a while. I lay in my bunk on the bus many a night and pondered days such as this one, January 9, 2010.

For me, it has already been a great couple of weeks at home, off the road. Lots of time spent with wife and family. In fact, a week ago I spent a whole day here at my farm with my grandchildren Breanne and Luke, four-wheeling all over the place while nearly freezing to death.

I have spent this week at home in Hendersonville, enjoying Mary's great cooking and, in turn, trying to take care of one honey-do list after another. Then yesterday I spent the afternoon with Dana Williams of the group Diamond Rio, recording interviews and such for his weekly online radio show. Dana and I are of like minds and spirit, and the show turned out really well. I was honored to be in his home and honored that he centered a whole show on Ban-Joey and the Oak Ridge Boys.

After that I headed out to my farm. The snow had begun to fall. I went to bed relatively early so I would rise at a good hour and be able to enjoy every bit of this day. I just knew this was going to be one of those special days, the kind of day one dreams about.

I awoke at 6:30 a.m. and watched the early morning arrive in the holler. Over 150 turkeys lined my front pasture. I put on a pot of

Dunkin' Donuts medium roast and watched as three coyotes appeared. I thought about hitting the gun safe and getting out my Ruger Range Rifle, but they were too far away for me to have ever gotten off a good shot. And besides, by the time I got back to the front porch, they would probably be gone.

I figured I was about to see a massacre through my binoculars, but it never materialized. The turkeys did not run or fly off but stood ground, and I guess it paid off because the coyotes just padded around them and eventually went away.

Then the deer came. Last night before settling in I had put some corn out for them, and there were six does dining in the same front pasture where the turkeys still hunkered down.

I drank coffee and picked on my Gibson Grenada for about two hours as the snow continued to fall and the air continued to freeze. Then I bundled up good and went outside.

I fed my donkeys some sweet feed, and then started up my two John Deere tractors and my two JD Gators and let them run for a bit. They choked and sputtered some, but they eventually started on up and hummed along just fine. Like a farmer in Iowa once said, "You pay a little extra for that green paint, son, but you do want it to start up every morning, don't 'cha?"

Then I took a long walk. I carried with me a camera as well as my Taurus Judge sidearm, which fires either a forty-five caliber cartridge or a 410 shotgun shell. Like the ad says, "You be the judge!"

I usually just carry a Colt 380 or a Sturm Ruger Hammerless .38 out here, but with coyotes out and about in the daylight I was more comfortable with the Judge!

A note on what bundling up means on a day when the wind-chill factor is in single digits: Two sweatshirts, heavy socks, a Carthartt one-piece jumpsuit, a toasty warm camouflage coat with a hood, and, of course, boots, gloves, and a woolen toboggan hat. I looked ridiculous, but I was warm. If I were to be attacked by coyotes, I would be perfectly able to shoot them all long before they ever chewed through this stuff and got to any meat and bones.

I thought about two of my singing partners, William Lee Golden and Richard Sterban, who were both vacationing with their wives on the Sir Francis Drake Channel in the Virgin Islands. Their wind-chill factor was probably around seventy-five degrees right about then. I am certain they were having lots of fun!

For many years, Mary and I went to the Caribbean in January. But since we bought this farm over eleven years ago, we have not gone south for the winter. We have chosen to enjoy this instead. I may go back to St. Johns again one day, but for now I am very happy to be right here.

So for about three hours I walked along the creek, through field after snow-covered field, and through a bunch of woods as well. It was so quiet I could hear the busy beavers as they gnawed upon wood, a buck rubbing antlers against a tree, little birds flitting about, their wings fluttering in the quiet snowfall.

I could hear turkeys and hawks. I saw rabbits and does hopping through and above fence lines. But most of all I could see God in everything. I came home and took a long hot shower and made some soup. Then I picked my banjo for a few more hours and began to write this piece.

Banjo. Family. Farm. It seems at times that this is what I am all about. Add singing songs and writing words to the mix, and that is indeed what I have become. Not a bad place to be. As I wrote in a piece called *A Nothing Day*, it is important to be quiet and to do nothing on occasion so God can speak to your heart, and you can refuel your engine and get stronger.

I so needed a day like this. I think we all do.

God sometimes speaks to us in metaphors. As I stared across the snowy fields, I was reminded that because of Jesus Christ and the promise of John 3:16, my sins have become whiter than snow. Well, I assure you the snow that is still falling by my window is evermore white. This is white as God intended white to be. Think of something whiter than fresh-falling snow. Not possible, except for my many sins, of course. How amazing is that? This is unimaginable forgiveness!

Today I saw so many birds. There were bluebirds, cardinals, wrens, kingfishers, heron, meadowlarks, and sparrows of all kinds. Matthew 6:26 tells us to consider the birds. They do not sow nor reap nor do they store food in barns, and yet the heavenly Father feeds them!

How wonderful to know that God is out there and that He is always looking after us. Whether we are consumed with our work or our family or even by a quiet and peaceful day like today, His still, small voice is always speaking and teaching and witnessing to our very soul. We just have to be listening. Just what today has been all about.

As I sit here in this wonderful silence and continue to write, I am reminded of a great songwriter and poet I love by the name of Jesse Winchester. He once wrote a song called "Wintery Feeling."

Although I love the song, the overall message in the lyric would indicate that falling snow and a graying sky might put one in a frame of mind to write down something of a dark or lonely nature. I must differ a bit with this prolific poet because all this cold and snow is making me feel just great. I just could not wait to open up a fresh page and start to write down something that is positive and inspiring.

I am feeling so very blessed. Blessed with a great family. Blessed with love. Blessed with music, and blessed that God would give me a day like this to quietly praise Him and to thank Him for these blessings.

So I will lay my pen down now and enjoy the rest of the day. I will snack and pick and watch some football on TV. From time to time I will wrap myself up inside my huge John Deere fleece blanket and go outside and sit on my porch and stare out into the rare arctic freeze that has descended upon much of the USA.

Wintry feeling? I guess so, if that means blowing and freezing snow and sleet and a wind-chill factor of around four degrees. But down deep within the fibers of my being, I am warm as toast!

Soon the Oak Ridge Boys will be back to playing and singing and riding and planning our new year. We will talk creatively about this year's show and what songs we will sing and how we will sing them. We will talk of production and promotion and possible new recording projects. We will laugh, and we will enjoy being what and who we are. We have done this for decades and it never gets old!

There will soon come a night when Joey will be fast asleep in his bunk on a moving tour bus. The white lines will be flying beneath him, and the miles passing will eventually lead to another town and another show. He will be oblivious of this, however, for he will be dreaming of a wintry day when the snow is falling down upon his farm in the holler, and he is out there all alone with his thoughts while walking through fields and woods.

He will hear the soft rustle of an animal in the woods or the flutter of wings. He will hear the faraway cry of the red-tailed hawk, and he will feel the frigid air upon his face. He will stop by the creek and get lost in the sound of the moving water. He will eventually make his way up a logging trail that leads from the back woods to an upper pasture. He will make his way back to the warm log cabin, while stopping to take a picture or two.

He will picture himself all warm and toasty and clean and sitting on the couch picking some banjo while he watches the snow outside continue to fall . . .

BILLY'S TORNADO

A family story about a storm, faith, and miracles

For my precious and loving daughters,
Jennifer and Sabrina.
Also, for the lost—may they be found!

AUTHOR'S NOTE

The little story you are about to read, and all the characters within the confines of this inspirational children's story, are a figment of my imagination. However, the idea of a family of faith who has to cope with loss and disaster has become all too common of late.

Parts of my home counties of Sumner and Macon in the great State of Tennessee have been devastated by horrendous tornados that touched down and plowed a swath of horror through mile after mile of countryside and city alike. Thousands of homes were lost and many lost their lives in these storms. Many folks have not even been found and, unlike Billy's mom, may never be found.

In 2007 a tornado wiped out the whole town of Greensburg, Kansas, and other incredible events such as hurricanes, wildfires, and floods have been even more astounding. A few years ago a tsunami on the other side of the world took several hundred thousand lives, and recent earthquakes in Haiti and Chile caused more destruction.

Seeing things like tornados, hurricanes like Katrina, and even the evil terrorist attack of 9-11 through the medium of television does not give justice to the horror of such an event. We seem to be becoming desensitized by the constant barrage of twenty-four-hour news coverage.

"Oh look, hon, another hurricane! Wow, look at that! Pass the salt."

But for those local volunteers, as well as policemen, firemen, and emergency personnel who have to dig through the rubble to try to save a human life, it becomes all too real. The pit inside your gut and heart is immeasurable when you drive by what was once a home, a business, or a farm that is now gone from the planet. I take much comfort, though, when I see the human response in the face of such disaster. People are always ready to jump in and give of themselves to help their neighbor.

Most people will work and give until it hurts. In the old days we always heard about a barn raising when all of the farmers would gather up to help build a brother's barn that was blown down in a storm or burnt up in a fire. I have seen these kinds of men rebuild a house or a church today with the same fervor.

After a tragedy like the recent tornados in Tennessee, it is always a joy to see the Red Cross, the Salvation Army, and Feed the Children trucks come rolling in with food and supplies for the needy. There is always a blessing when one looks at the absolute good side of the American family, and it makes me very proud and honored to be living in these United States.

Your humble author has no idea what to really make of all of these storms that have hurt so many, no more than I understand the mind of the evildoer who would terrorize and kill innocent people. However, as a Christian I do know this much: We must certainly turn our eyes upon Jesus.

Only a childlike faith in Him can bring us through whatever this world has in store for us. There will always be death and destruction of one kind or another until that day when Jesus Christ splits the eastern sky and returns to take all of us who trust in Him to heaven. That event will make even an F-5 tornado seem pretty lame.

We just have to continue to learn to trust in Him and have faith in Him and to praise Him in all things. Only God knows the reasons. We also must take a hard look in the mirror and come to realize how very small we are when compared to the heavens.

This book is more of a children's book and, as you know, a children's book always has a happy ending. But to get to that happy ending the Lyons family's faith had to be tested. A little boy had to learn the importance of life even as he faced his own possible death and the possible loss of his mother.

At this writing there are many who have lost homes and loved ones right here in my hometown, and I do grieve and pray for them and their families. But know this. For those of us who accept Jesus Christ into our heart as our very personal Savior, for those of us who will put Him first in our lives, for those of us who will walk the narrow road of righteousness and forsake evil, I assure you that one day we will find ourselves in the presence of God's holy angels, and our souls will be bathed in the everlasting light and love of God's only Son! There will be no more sickness or pain or loss.

Let this thought bring to you some joy amongst the tragedies!

God bless you one and all, and thanks for reading.

BILLY'S TORNADO

For I reckon that the sufferings of this present time are not worthy to be compared with the glory, which shall be revealed in us.

—Romans 8:18

L ittle Billy Lyons had been fast asleep in his bed just moments before a huge train seemed to rumble right on through his house. An evil train that would destroy almost every single thing he and his family owned. One would certainly think there was a certain amount of safety in being inside one's own room, nestled deep within one's Indianapolis Colts oversized fleece blanket. But on this night of nights very few were safe from the thunder and utter chaos that seemed to descend from the sky like some sort of monster. It was, in fact, a terrible storm that would change the lives of the Lyons family forever.

Billy and his mom and dad had moved to the Midwest from California last year, and everything seemed to be working out well for the Lyons family. Billy's dad was a construction engineer, and it was not hard for him to latch onto a new and good-paying job. The world was growing every day, and there was always a need for a man who knew how to build things.

Billy's mom was a pre-school teacher, and the Antioch Baptist Church had a great pre-school program where she fit in immediately. The slower-paced lifestyle was a welcome change from the hectic and traffic-ridden area of the country where the Lyons family had lived before. Besides all that, his mom was especially tired of forest fires, mudslides, and earthquakes. Getting out of southern California just seemed like a good idea.

Their timing was great as well from a financial standpoint. They were able to sell their modest home in California and build a much nicer, two story home here—and still have money left over to put away for Billy's future and perhaps a few extras. Dad still drove his old Ford Bronco, but mom ended up with a new GM Saturn and just loved it.

I guess they never really put much thought into a possible tornado. In fact, a tornado never even crossed their mind. It had been such a good day too, especially for Billy. The sun was shining brightly and the weather seemed really warm for this time of the year. Billy was able to wear the Indianapolis Colts windbreaker he had received for Christmas for the very first time, and he showed it off to all of his classmates with pride.

He also brought home a great report card, and his mom and dad were very proud of him. All A's and just one C in math, but Billy promised he would do better on that one. (Although he really wasn't sure he could. Math just seemed so hard for him.)

His dad told him that it would get even harder as he progressed to middle school and high school—and eventually college. That thought almost made him sick on his stomach because in his mind all mathematics pretty much sucked! Besides, what did math have to do with football?

Billy loved football. His room was adorned with all kinds of Colts stuff. In fact, one whole wall was devoted to a life-sized Peyton Manning that just stuck there like magic. The giant Peyton was a Christmas gift from his dad. It stretched from floorboard to ceiling and Billy loved it. He also adored the Colts, and he was not even sure why.

There was no NFL team in Southern California to cheer for, and he didn't like the Raiders or Forty-Niners much. But somehow he took a liking to the Colts, and now they owned his complete love and dedication. They rewarded Billy by actually winning the Super Bowl over da Bears, which was very cool.

Billy was not a very big boy, but he had a ton of heart. He had played Little League football for several years now, and he was a darn good player. He prayed every night that God would help him to grow bigger and stronger so that one day he could play for Indianapolis.

On the night the train came Billy was dreaming that he was on an NFL practice field and, as a wide receiver, he was running pass routes.

Peyton Manning would drop back from behind the center and hit him right on the numbers in full stride no matter which way he would cut and run. Let's face it, man, Peyton is the best quarterback who has ever lived. Oh, Tom Brady was pretty good too, and there were some other guys coming along like Leinart and Young. But Peyton just had to be . . .

"BILLY! Wake up, son! I mean RIGHT NOW!"

Billy was already in the wake-up mode because he could hear Jack barking somewhere outside. That was strange because usually at night Jack was asleep at the foot of the bed. Jack was a three-year-old Irish setter that made the trip to the Midwest with the Lyons family.

Man, that trip was a doozy, thought Billy. *Jack actually peed inside the Bronco once and Mom threatened to throw him out the window in some town named Tucumcari, New Mexico. Dad laughed for a hundred miles.*

Dad was not laughing now!

"Come on, son, put some clothes on and come with me. There is a big storm heading this way."

Billy jumped out of bed and started to quickly take off his pajamas and get into his jeans and sweatshirt. He was shaking a bit. The tone of his dad's voice actually scared him. A storm was coming?

"Where is Mom?" Billy asked as he tied up his sneakers.

"She is looking after the horses. Let's roll, pal. She will meet us in the basement."

Moments before, his dad had been sitting in the living room watching television. Like most men he was not content to stay committed to a single channel for very long. With the remote control in one hand and a hot cup of his wife's special chamomile tea in the other, he would search through a good mix of news, sports, and movies. Billy's mom, reading a new Max Lucado inspirational book while nestled in her favorite chair by her favorite lamp, just couldn't' take it anymore.

"Honey, will you please stop it? You are driving me nuts with that thing."

"Not a long drive either!" he answered with a laugh.

She scowled at him, but he knew she really wasn't mad. He knew how to push the envelope, and he also knew when to put on the brakes. That was called marriage and he did, in fact, love and adore this wonderful woman.

By then a pretty decent rainstorm was going on outside, and the wind was starting to have a bit of a kick to it. "Put on the local news or weather, hon," she said. "I don't like the sound of that storm out there."

Billy's dad flipped to the local news station. There before them was the storm tracker radar showing red and purple colors all over the screen. It seemed a huge front was coming through very quickly and tornado warnings were in effect for—

Just then loud sirens began to wail from nearby, as the weather person was giving instructions. "This is not a watch—it is a warning, which means that tornados have been spotted in the following counties. You are urged to go to your basement immediately. Stay away from glass. Do not go outside!"

Billy's dad was on it. "I will grab a flashlight and go get Billy!"

His mom headed for the side door just as Jack came bounding down the stairs from Billy's room. Barking loudly, he followed her out the door.

"Where are you going?" Billy's dad yelled franticly.

"I want to secure the horses. I will meet you in the basement!"

"But, honey—"

"I will be fine. I have to look after Puff and Stuff. Get Billy downstairs. I will be there in a shake."

One of the real perks of owning a bit of land was being able to own two beautiful horses. Billy's mom had loved horses from the time she was little, but she grew up in a city where there was no room to accommodate her dream. With Jack at her side, she ran the fifty yards to the barn and opened up the big door. Puff and Stuff were each in their stalls, and she just wanted to make sure that—

The tornado came without warning. She heard the deafening roar behind her as she opened the barn door. She turned around, and what she saw through the pouring rain was like a nightmare. This thing was right above her house and churning it to pieces. She ran back towards the house screaming. Jack was still right on her heels barking loudly.

Billy's dad had scooped him up in his arms and carried him down to the basement. There was a full bathroom, surrounded by a cinderblock wall. His dad would come home from work on some nights, enter the basement through a side entrance at the bottom of a stairwell, and then shower down here before going upstairs.

As they entered the little protected room Billy asked, "Where is Mom?"

"She will be here in a minute, son. That woman and her horses—"

At that very moment in time and space, the train came. At least that is what it sounded like. It was a very loud train. Louder than anything Billy or his father had ever heard.

Billy's dad grabbed him and held him close. He sat down hard and leaned against a wall while all hell broke loose above them. Breaking glass, cracking wood, falling trees. It sounded like the end of the world, and perhaps it was. The pressure behind their eyes and inside their ears was maddening. It felt like the tornado was on them for hours when, in fact, it had only been about thirty seconds. Then a complete and eerie silence enveloped them.

Billy and his dad began to slowly pick up the sounds of crying and sobbing as their hearing returned, and quickly realized the sounds were actually coming from themselves. Billy's dad stood up and looked around the basement.

There were two windows in the basement, and they were both shattered and sort of caved in. The stairwell that lead to the upstairs was also caved in so there was no way to get back up into the house. The outside stairwell that led up and out of the basement was covered up in debris, including what was left of a huge oak tree that had stood like a huge sentinel right beside the driveway.

They called out as loud as they could for Billy's mom, but no answer returned to them. Except for a few distant sounds of sirens there was only silence. They were trapped in this basement and would be for the rest of this night on into late morning.

Billy's dad was sobbing and whispering his wife's name when little Billy snapped him out of it. "We need to pray. Dad, we really need to pray!"

"Yes we do, son. I believe our faith is about to tested." His dad was still sobbing as he spoke.

Billy's dad tried to gather himself a bit, but it was difficult to do so. Yes, he was a man of faith. Yes, he was a born-again Christian, but his heart was still full of fear. Fear for his wife and fear for so many others in this wonderful little town who had welcomed his family with love and friendship.

He once again pulled his son toward him and hugged him. "I am not sure what we will find up above us, Billy. I fear our house is gone. But you know that is just fine. I can build it back up easy as pie. What really matters is that you are okay, and we need to pray that your mother is okay as well. I don't know what I would do without her. We had better pray for our friends and neighbors as well, son."

Billy and his dad got down on their knees in what was left of their basement and prayed. They prayed for Billy's mother, for their neighbors, for their church and they even sent up a few flares for Jack and for Puff and Stuff.

"It will be fine, son. God is in control. We must lean on Him no matter what. No matter what!"

They had both fallen into a deep sleep when the sounds of chainsaws and shouting voices awakened them. "Anybody down there?"

"Yes, yes we are here, my son and I! We are okay, but my wife is missing. Would you check the barn, please!" *If it is still there.*

The barn was still there. The house was gone, but the barn was still there as if nothing had happened. A bunch of good old boys from town sawed that fallen tree to pieces in no time, and then National Guardsmen and a few deputies from the sheriff's department helped dig Billy and his dad out of the basement.

The damage to the house was incredible. The roof was gone, and all four walls had been turned inside out as if a bomb had been dropped on it. The big oak had also taken out the new GM Saturn Billy's mom had parked in the driveway. It was crushed like a toy.

Billy's dad wandered around the barn looking for signs of his wife. The horses were just fine. His Ford Bronco was just fine. Thankfully, he always parked it in the barn. Beyond his property he could see the where the tornado had been. The morning sun had now risen pretty high in the eastern sky, and it did a nice job of illuminating the storm's pathway. He could see at least four other homes that had been severely damaged, but he had no idea the extent of the damage until he met with Sheriff Burke about an hour later.

"Around two hundred homes are gone and twenty people dead so far. The county hospital is full of injured people, and I am afraid the morgue is filling up as well. So far we have around seventeen folks missing and unaccounted for, and I have put your wife's name on that list. I am so sorry. They say this is the worst storm to ever hit this part of the state."

"What about my mom?" Billy asked.

"We will have hundreds of men out looking for the missing, Billy. We have all kinds of volunteers, National Guardsmen and law enforcement officers. I have never seen so many badges in my entire life!"

"What do we do now?" asked Billy's dad.

"The Feds are already sending disaster aid. They are setting up a row of trailers within a few days down by Sutter's farm, which was spared. If your insurance doesn't provide a place for you to stay until a lot of this shakes out, you can line up for one of those. Or perhaps you can spend a few nights with Mrs. Burke and me."

"Thanks, sheriff. That is very kind of you. We still have our Bronco so we can dig a few things out of the wreckage and head for a motel somewhere, or perhaps we can bunk out in the barn until you find my wife. Right now though I want to get to our church."

"Um, which church is that?" asked Sheriff Burke.

"Antioch Baptist," Billy answered.

"I am afraid it is gone."

Our church is gone too. Billy almost started crying again, but he held back his tears. He did not want to weep like a little boy in front of Sheriff Burke.

"Listen," added the sheriff, "the Red Cross and Salvation Army as well as Feed the Children are already setting up in the middle of town. They have blankets and clothes and hot meals. Get on down there and get something to eat. There will be no power or cell phone service around here for a few days so keep checking in with my office."

The first thing they did was start up the Bronco and take a ride. It was amazing. You could drive down the main road and everything would look normal for a while, and then all of a sudden there was a path of total destruction. So many homes and farms and even a good part of downtown had been flattened like a pancake. Business establishments of all kinds were now piles of rubble.

It was hard getting through roadblocks, but being a storm victim carried weight with the authorities. His dad had dug out a beautiful picture of his mom, and he was showing it to everyone. In the coming days he and Billy would be busy helping lots of people, while at the same time praying with them and for them. But first they took the sheriff's advice and went to the Feed the Children headquarters on the west side of town. Right beside a truck where they were serving hot meals there was a huge Colts logo. To Billy's surprise there were actually several Indianapolis Colt players handing out food.

As they got closer they noticed one rather tall man talking to a bunch of kids and handing them bottles of water. Billy could not believe it. It was Peyton Manning! Billy ran right up to him and extended his hand.

"Hello, Mr. Manning. I am Billy. You are my favorite player in the whole world. We lost our home and we cannot find my mom and my dog and I even lost all of my Colts stuff and—"

The big quarterback knelt down by Billy and gave him a big hug.

"I am so sorry, Billy. But I promise you that God has a plan and a reason for all of this. I'll be praying hard that they find your mom."

Through his tears Billy said, "Then I can get back to football because, you see, I am a wide receiver, and someday I may play for the Colts too."

Billy's dad walked up to the star quarterback and shook his hand. "Thank you," he said.

"Not a problem. We just want to try to help out some. Has the boy ever been to a Colts game?"

"No, he hasn't."

"Well here, take this card. When things settle down, I want you to call this number. You can be my guest next season."

"That is very kind of you. Thanks for being here."

"Your wife is in my prayers, sir."

After a hot meal served up by Feed the Children and some of the Indianapolis Colts, Billy, and his father drove to the church.

The red brick building of the Antioch Baptist church was gone. A few piles of rubble were all that was left. There was nobody there at the moment, but over the next few days many able bodied men, including Billy's dad, would be helping to clean up the debris.

A handmade sign hung on what was left of a doorframe simply read: Service this Sunday morning at 11 a.m. Please attend. Rev. Hatcher.

"Thank you, Lord," Billy whispered.

Next, they drove to Sheriff Burke's office to fill out paperwork. There was still no word on Billy's mom. Then they took a trip to the local State Farm Insurance office. That place was really busy, however, it seemed that plenty of extra folks were on hand to help the victims of the storm.

After even more paperwork and assurances from the agent in charge that everything was covered, they drove about sixty miles to a Days Inn that had a room available. After a stop at Wal-mart for snacks and some extra clothes, Billy and his dad knelt beside their rented twin beds and asked the Lord to bless all of those who were hurting—and to please bring Billy's mom back home.

It took a while for Billy to fall asleep. There was so much to process, and he was still just a boy. He had lost his home, and his church had blown down. His mom and dog were who knows where, and he had actually met Peyton Manning. Even with all of that Billy fell into a deep and dreamless sleep.

Billy's dad stared at the ceiling for a long while as well. What would he ever do without his precious wife? How could he even get through a day without her being at his side? They had met in college, and for him it had been love at first sight. It took another few days for her, but she had eventually come around. The thought made him smile. *Oh God, please bring her back to me.* Then he also fell into a merciful sleep.

The next several days were somewhat of a blur to Billy Lyons and his dad. Driving out of town was certainly easier than driving back home. The roads were full of electric service trucks from all over the state as well as Guardsmen and emergency vehicles. Adding to the chaos and congestion were radio and TV people from everywhere. CNN and Fox News were even here. It was rumored that the president of the United States was coming for a visit.

They managed to evade all of this and made their way on through town. The Feed the Children truck was still there, but it seemed the Colts players were now gone. Billy wondered if they were ever there.

That part seemed a lot like one of his crazy dreams. They made their way through the same roadblocks and headed toward what had been their home.

While they were sifting through the rubble, Billy's dad's cell phone chirped. It was a goofy bird sound that sounded quite distinctive. The caller ID screen indicated the sheriff's office.

"Hello, sheriff."

"Just checking on you. Cell phone service seems to be back in order. Listen, I took the liberty to um, well, check the morgue and check through the entire hospital, and there is no sign of your wife anywhere."

'Thank you very much, Sheriff Burke. That was a very nice thing for you to do."

"I could say that it is my job, but you know it is more than that. We have a lot to deal with around here, my friend, but we are still looking for her. You boys okay?"

"We are fine."

"Well, call me if you need me."

Click. Just like that, Sheriff Burke was gone.

There was a forty-acre pasture behind the Lyons home and barn, and Billy decided to take a long walk while his dad and other men were working on the mess. There was tons of stuff out there, and he wanted to see it all up close.

There were pieces of pink and yellow insulation everywhere. He found clothing and pieces of siding and hunks of roof wherever he walked. He actually found someone's checkbook. He didn't know the person, but he decided to save it and try to get it back to him.

As he walked the entire distance of the field he noticed something blue on a lower branch of a tree. He ran to it and discovered his Colts fleece blanket suspended there. He jumped up and pulled it down and wrapped it around his shoulders. It was then that he was struck with an agonizing and almost obvious thought. His mother had been taken up in the storm and so had Jack. This awful tornado plucked up his mom and his dog, just like in some weird storybook thing, and took them somewhere and let them go—just like his blanket and the man's checkbook. He sat down by the tree and wept and prayed for his precious mother.

By Sunday the county had restored power and things had settled down. Bulldozers could be heard everywhere. Cleanup was well on its way, and soon the rebuilding process would begin. Everywhere you looked it seemed that people had accepted what happened and were more than ready to get to work and put the awful twister behind them.

Hundreds of people gathered at the Antioch Baptist Church on Sunday morning. They sat in folding chairs beneath a big tree about twenty-five yards from where the church had stood. All the rubble was gone, although the huge white steeple still rested on its side in the parking lot. Billy and his father sat side by side about halfway back from the small lectern, where the ministry of music was now leading the congregation in singing that great hymn, "Leaning on the Everlasting Arms."

There was no piano or organ, but several boys not much older than Billy were strumming on acoustic guitars. It was a beautiful sound. It was the sound of God's people honoring and praising Him even in the face of immeasurable pain and sacrifice and loss. Everyone sitting there knew in their hearts that they were very blessed just to be there. Many of their friends were not.

It was a humbling and blessed time for this congregation, and as Reverend Hatcher said in his sermon, "A church is not made of brick and mortar. That is just a building. The heart of the church is its people. A church is made up of souls who belong to God, not just a bunch of stones and a steeple. A house is rubble to begin with if God doesn't dwell in its inhabitants. For a house to be a home there has to be love and, my friends, I assure you that there is no greater love today than the love of our Savior Jesus Christ.

"We must lean on His everlasting arms in this time of challenge and loss. We must pray as Jesus did in the garden, not my will be done but Thy will be done. Then we must learn to accept the fact that His will may be different than our own. Therefore our faith will be tested, yet rewarded when we indeed learn to lay all of our burdens and cares upon Him.

"He has told us in His word to do so and, my friends, this is what we must do. Lean upon Him! Give Him your heart. We will rebuild this church and we will rebuild our homes. Our lost loved ones will be missed, but because of Christ and His death on the cross, we have the assurance that we will see them once again."

The sermon was interrupted by the sound of Sheriff Burke's car as he pulled into the lot and just touched his siren for a second. The sheriff jumped out of the car and in one sweeping motion opened up the back door. Billy turned to see what the commotion was all about. He could not believe what his eyes told him. With a little help from Sheriff Burke, a woman rose shakily from the back seat of the patrol car.

It was his mother!

"Mom!" He cried as he ran to her outstretched arms. She gathered him up in a warm mother's embrace and rocked him back and forth. Her face was scratched up, and she had bandages on both arms and both legs. But nothing was broken and she looked just . . .

"Beautiful." Billy's dad said as he appeared behind him. "The most beautiful sight I have ever seen."

She reached out one arm and gathered her husband in as well. "My sweet darling, I love you so much," she whispered.

"I love you. I just knew that God would bring you back to me."

There was much praise and rejoicing in that little makeshift church on that Sunday morning. There was singing and dinner on the grounds and at the end of the day nobody wanted to leave. These fine folks, who had been through so much in the past week, had just seen a miracle, and it gave them all the faith and courage to lick their wounds and get on with their lives.

Billy's mom explained her story. She had seen the tornado descend upon their home and remembered running. It was a blur, but she must have been pulled up and into the storm. All she remembered was a loud roar and being lifted up into the air. She awoke in old man Braddock's farmhouse with Mrs. Braddock looking after her.

"They had no power or phone, and they are elderly so there was no way I could get word to you. When the sheriff got around to checking on them he found me there. I am so thankful to have survived that awful thing. I never stopped praying my heart out for you both."

"We prayed our hearts out for you too, Mom." Billy said. "And by the way, the barn came out okay, and old Puff and Stuff are just fine.

"You'll be back riding in no time," Billy's father said. He was not able to wipe that happy grin off his face.

Just then Sheriff Burke came over.

"I have more great news. The county animal shelter just called. It seems they have found a big yellow setter with a collar that says 'Jack' just as big and bold as can be."

Everyone cheered as the Lyons family climbed into the Ford Bronco and headed out of the parking lot. Billy's dad drove over to their property and slowly pulled the old Bronco into the driveway. The Lyons family sat there in silence for a long while and gazed upon the mess that was once their home.

"You can rebuild it, huh, Dad?" Billy asked.

"Yes I can, son. Better than it was!"

He put his arm around his wife and held her close.

"My poor car," she said.

"We will get another one, my dear."

"What's next?" she asked.

"Well, we check on Puff and Stuff, and then drive over and pick up Jack. Then we head for the Days Inn, where we now reside," he chuckled.

"No, I mean what is next, overall? I mean, how long before we have a home again?"

"Well, it is like Reverend Hatcher said earlier. We will always have a home right here in our hearts. We are so very blessed, for we have each other. But to really answer your question, sweet wife, my plan is to have us up and running again before fall. Then, we have a Colts game to go to!"

"Yeah!" said Billy.

The end? No way! A beginning!